SMALLCREEP'S DAY

Peter Currell Brown wrote *Smallcreep's Day* while working in a Gloucestershire factory. Its success enabled him to give up factory work and realise his dream of setting up a craft pottery in rural Gloucestershire. Since then he has been involved in a series of craft enterprises in various parts of the country. He now lives and works in woodlands near Sherwood Forest making spinning-wheels for enthusiasts and museums.

SMALLCREEP'S DAY

Peter Currell Brown

PINTER & MARTIN

Smallcreep's Day

First published by Victor Gollancz Ltd 1965
This edition published by Pinter & Martin Ltd 2008

Copyright © Peter Currell Brown 1965, 2008

ISBN 978-1-905177-15-8

The right of Peter Currell Brown to be identified as the author of this work
has been asserted by him in accordance with the Copyright, Designs
and Patent Act of 1988

British Library Cataloguing-in-Publication Data
A catalogue record for this book is available from the British Library

Set in Sabon

Printed in Great Britain by
CPD, Wales

Pinter & Martin Ltd
6 Effra Parade
London SW2 1PS

www.pinterandmartin.com

I pulled myself up. 'Now surely, Smallcreep,' I said to myself, 'you are having difficulty in distinguishing the real from the fantastic, from strange dreams inside your own head.' But if the real is also fantastic, how is one supposed to tell the difference? I only know that it is useless to say to myself that such-and-such was fantasy, and was, therefore, not real, when there it was as clear as my own hand in front of me. If I have seen a corpse working a machine, then what use is it to tell myself that I imagined it? I saw it. If I have seen crowds of men handcuffed together who shouted continuously that they were free, and I spoke to them and touched their handcuffs, what use is it to say, 'No, this is hallucination or exaggeration, it is not to be believed'? If both true and false are often equally unbelievable, how shall I distinguish them? If I do distinguish them, may I not in the process become astounded by real things which I had hitherto regarded as perfectly normal, or be completely confused by what I had previously understood and taken for granted? Perhaps I should become utterly terrified by things which had been accepted by everyone who knew about them as perfectly ordinary and harmless. I was in no state for that kind of business, and resolved to leave such details for other people to puzzle out.

chapter one

It was late that morning when I moved out of our particular small corner of bearable noise into the body of the factory. The previous evening I had asked my wife to pack me extra sandwiches. This she had done, and had cut the bread and cheese with great generosity – Swiss cheese, which she knows I am very fond of, and bacon fried crisp and allowed to go cold. These I now carried in a knapsack over my shoulder, and in my right-hand pocket was an unopened tin of my usual pipe-tobacco.

I strode forward with what was, I fancy now, a rather exaggerated determination, for I was secretly a little apprehensive. George and Frank, whom I left behind in the slotting section to look after matters while I was away, were completely baffled by my escapade and said so; but I knew that they were very capable men with nearly a century of service to the firm between them, and that they were completely trustworthy. No, I had no anxieties about what I was leaving behind me; it was what lay ahead – all nonsense really, after all, I had worked here in this section of the factory for sixteen years; and yet in all that time I had not been very far from my machine in any direction. There was never any need to, you see; besides, we were busy and I had never had the time. Some of the men, I know, found important looking pieces of paper from time to time in the waste bins and would go walking off carrying them, to show anyone who might stop them. They often came back with strange stories of what they had seen in various parts of the factory, and one or two never came back at all. But, for myself, I believed none of the stories and regarded these men as irresponsible loiterers, capable of any amount of lying. But all those years I had had a secret yearning to know this one particular fact, a yearning which had recently grown so much in intensity that I could neither sleep, nor work, nor eat, nor play with my children: so that I had become no better than a burden to my family and friends and feared that I must fast be becoming a liability to my employers. The question had to be answered; and then the pressure of work eased off, so that I had resolved to set out to find that answer.

I strode between the rows of huge machines. Row upon row came towards me like the waves of the sea which seem to come from the horizon. Soon our own small section of four machines was far behind me, and the noise had risen to a pitch which I found quite painful. I had expected this. I think there can be no noise on earth like the noise of a factory. It is similar to the noise of a talking crowd, in that although one can hear every single syllable uttered one cannot distinguish any separate word. I know the noise of a lathe very well, indeed, I can distinguish a Parkson from a Colchester with no difficulty; I can recognise the sound of a vertical borer and can distinguish it from a horizontal borer; likewise with centred and centreless grinders, shapers and planers, single and multiple-spindled drilling machines, and so on. It is, I should think, rather like bird-spotting. The metal being cut in all these different ways makes sounds very like birds. On the shaper it caws like a persistent crow; pins and small punches being ground sound exactly like quarrelling sparrows, but more regular. Most machines squawk and screech and scream like the parrot house at the zoo, but the parrots all make quite different noises too, I imagine. But now that I was surrounded on all sides and overwhelmed by these machines and many others which I knew, I could hear none of them. There was only a ceaseless roar, which seemed to impinge on the mind not only by way of the ears, but through the nose and mouth and scalp also. I felt contained in some kind of jelly of sound, difficult to walk through and difficult to breathe, even difficult to see through. But I was quite familiar with all this, and had come prepared. I stopped, opened my knapsack and drew out a quantity of cotton wool. This I pushed carefully into each ear. Relief was instantaneous and I strode on, much comforted.

I was also prepared for the next source of discomfort, which was a matter of eyes rather than ears. As I looked around me I saw eyes which stared at me as I passed. They peered from between machines and from the depths of cupboards, from wastebins and from heaps of engine components. They stared through the sooty glass hatches of minute green tin offices, they popped up suddenly over vertical borers, and followed my movement from beneath the beds of great presses. They ranged in rows along the edges of greasy benches. Several pairs suddenly appeared in the darkness beneath a grating under my feet, so that for a moment I was afraid that I might step on them. This phenomenon, peculiar to factories and often remarked upon with concern by visitors to these places, was, I knew, attributable to nothing supernatural or more sinister than the lack of sufficient diversion in factory life; so that any new face or unusual occurrence draws the attention of every worker within sight of it. The fact that it is bad manners to stare is very well known to all these people, who would beat their children and divorce their wives for doing it, just like you and me; but inside a factory one cannot afford to miss anything which might be interesting or significant, and so I told myself that this was in fact a kind of compliment to me: I was considered interesting and possibly significant, and being so seldom considered to be either by anyone who knew me, I resolved to smile courteously at all these people who did not. In a very short time, however, I learned something of the difficulties which members of the royal family must face when appearing in public. Rejecting the idea of a fixed smile, I resolved to look ahead of me, so that I should offend none by preference.

I came to a place where a gangway crossed my own, and, striding across it with my eyes and ears thus preoccupied, I was knocked down by a small runabout truck. The driver stopped the truck, jumped down and sprinted over towards me with great excitement. I was about to apologise, to thank him for his concern and to reassure him that I was unhurt, when he ran past me and began to pick up my sandwiches, which had sprayed out of my knapsack on to the grimy floor. As fast as he could pick them up he stuffed them into his mouth, and in a few seconds my lunch was gone. He then came over to me, gesticulating like a windmill and moving his lips at me. I groped in my ears with the fingers of both hands, but my earplugs seemed to have retreated into my ears. I groped harder. He came and put his face very close to mine, chewing and champing with his jaw and speaking with his lips so that small pieces of cheese and bread jumped out at me from his mouth. From time to time a tiny slice of onion (which my wife must have slipped in as a surprise for me) came into my view as the food rotated in his mouth in the manner of a cement-mixer. I dug for the earplugs, for I was sure that he was saying something important. But then he punched me on the nose, and in a flash of light I realised that he must think that I was pushing my fingers in my ears in order not to hear him. Before I could explain he had remounted his truck and driven off, leaving behind him a cloud of blue smoke.

I was determined to have the earplugs out before doing anything else. I ignored the forest of eyes, and, getting down on hands and knees, searched about under a nearby bench for a piece of wire. There were five eyes under there. Why five I did not know and did not bother to ask, but groped about for wire. I disturbed a large black beetle which scuttled off, with a gait which was remarkably expressive of indignation for an insect, into an old tin from which it made a scrabbling noise at me. There were some cigarette ends and one or two old pieces of toenail there, and then I touched a piece of wire. It was rusty and very twisted, but it was good wire.

I rose and stood in the centre of the corridor where the light was a little better, and spent some time straightening the wire. Then I bent its end round to form a tiny hook, and began to feel around in my left ear. Just then a man in grey overalls came running with extraordinary speed down the corridor and pushed past me roughly without pausing and ran on. I repositioned the wire and tried again. Just as I felt the hook lodge itself in the cotton wool five more men came speeding down the corridor, one of them turning somersaults in his flight. They seemed not to see me and sent me staggering. I was determined not to lose my hold on the cotton wool, but with my arm raised in this position I was spun round like a top by a dozen or so more men who then appeared, some running and some leaping like hares. Hardly had these passed when I was overwhelmed by a great horde of charging men. As I was tossed about among them, gripping my earwire with determination, I saw that some were tumbling and somersaulting, some rolling like footballs along the ground, others running swiftly on their hands. Some bounced along on their stomachs, some cartwheeled and others flew through the air feet first or upside down, flapping their arms like birds and cannoning off their companions like pingpong balls. I was tossed about, sometimes on my head and sometimes on my feet, often colliding with men, whose lips moved briefly in a curse at each impact; but I clung on to my earwire throughout and when at last they had all passed, and I sat on the floor dazed, it was with the certain knowledge that I was in a position to withdraw my left earplug.

But I hesitated. On either side of me now were machines which were strange to me. Some had great clusters of trombone-like objects all over them, others had enormous wheels sticking out which were all covered in what looked like hundreds of burglar alarms. One machine which towered above me was crowned by a great circle of monstrous sledgehammers on long arms, all ranged about, so it seemed to me, so that the hammers would swing inwards to strike what looked like a vast upturned churchbell in the centre. What dreadful noises would such machines be making, I thought. I had heard of factories where it was necessary to wear earplugs all the time, and where not to do so would result in some kind of permanent aural injury. Perhaps this was such a place. But my nose had begun to smart, and I thought it better to try to establish contact with my fellow men, so I withdrew the left earplug slowly and tentatively and was amazed to hear no sound at all, save the occasional booming of the corrugated iron roof far above my head. I looked up and saw it rising and falling with the wind outside, but it was so dark up there and the roof so far away that I couldn't decide if this was in any way unusual or dangerous. Every machine was at rest. Then I noticed that the eyes had gone, every pair of them. I was alone. Now this was strange and rather frightening, and all sorts of alarming ideas rattled through my mind. Perhaps there was about to be an earthquake, or a nuclear war, and everyone had gone home to die in the arms of their wives. Perhaps there was a hurricane sweeping through the factory, or a fire. I listened again, but there was only the muffled booming of the roof. I fancied I could hear someone whistling in the distance, but wasn't sure. The most sensible thing would be to follow on in the direction the others had gone, I told myself. I began to walk.

I found it very strange and rather pleasant to walk between machines which were completely silent. There was the occasional quiet hiss of a leaky airline, the gentle thump-thump of a motor which someone had left idling, and my own footsteps. It was rather like walking in a museum among stuffed mammoths and dinosaurs. The wind outside must have dropped for the roof had stopped booming. I passed a clocking-in machine which click-clocked at me, and a tea-geyser which dripped and fussed down its brass tap. I came to a little green office no bigger than a sentry-box, and peeped in through its tiny window which was almost entirely covered with dusty old coloured postcards depicting fat women in embarrassing situations. The office was empty. I walked on a little more quickly now. To comfort myself I read out loud some of the notices which I passed. This factory abounds with notices and posters, some of them very, very old. Those in this part of it seemed more up-to-date, and cleaner. 'No stacking beyond this point,' I said timidly. Then, much louder, 'Spitting spreads disease,' followed up with 'Have you had the first component checked?' and 'Payment will be made only for time registered.' This last appeared on a clocking-in machine, and I went up close to it to read the smaller type. This said, 'Clocking in another man's card constitutes a fraud, and persons defrauding the Company will be prosecuted with a view to obtaining the maximum penalty.' I read this over once or twice in order to commit it to memory, then turned to continue walking. Just as I did so I thought I saw, some distance down the corridor, a dark figure which immediately disappeared to the right. The solitude must have been disturbing me, because instantly I broke into a run without thinking. I stopped and said to myself, 'You are not a shipwrecked mariner or a lost explorer. You are walking about in a factory in England and all things have a rational explanation.' But I could not make myself go slower than a brisk walk, and I reached the spot in a few minutes. There was a door there, at the side of the corridor. It was painted dark green, but was very dirty. From underneath it spread a sort of slimy dampness which extended for a few feet up and down the gangway. I thought for a moment, but the silence was too much. I knocked quietly on the door, which opened to reveal first total darkness, then the smallest room I have ever seen, and then the fact that I was looking at another door. I stepped inside the first to examine the second, whereupon the first slammed and I was left in the dark. There was a sliminess under my feet and an unpleasant smell. I knocked on the second door, and since there was no reply I felt for the knob. There was no knob so I just pushed.

I was looking into what seemed at first sight to be some kind of canteen. It was full of tobacco smoke and men, but there was no furniture, so that the men sat or crouched or lay on the wet floor. The room was very large, like a long hall, and almost every square foot of the floor was covered by men. They all munched at sandwiches and the air was full of the noise of champing teeth. Some were reading scraps of newspaper which looked as if they had been picked up from the floor, holding them close to their faces in the dim light. I looked up to the high roof and saw that it was made mostly of a kind of frosted glass, which was so caked with streaks and patches of greenish dust or mould that very little light was let in. Ferns and all manner of fungi and lichens hung down from the upper parts of the walls, which ran with brownish droplets of water. And there were pipes, such pipes as I'd never seen in my life. They covered the walls, travelling in every possible direction, weaving and crisscrossing in dazzling patterns. They were of every conceivable size and pattern and colour. There were heavy pipes with big fat joins every few feet like giant bamboo, gregarious pipes mooching across the walls in gangs, brisk businesslike shortest-distance-between-two-points pipes, big rusty iron pipes with wide bolted flanges along them, like rows of top hats. There were pipes which nipped off suddenly to right or left to speak to others for a moment before continuing on their original courses, and pipes which branched and branched and branched again for the sheer joy of multiplication, and forgot where they were going and got lost; and there was one old pipe as thick as a man's thigh which traced its way carefully round three walls of the room, paying particular attention to the corners, only to turn back, retrace its steps completely and disappear sadly through the same hole in the wall from whence it came. You could tell the old ones, which were straight because they were there first, whereas the new pipes bustled irritably around all the others or wandered leisurely about adjusting themselves as they went. There were green pipes, blue pipes, red pipes, pipes once painted white, even a square pipe and one that changed colour three times and then stopped halfway across a wall. And all were dripping and streaming with condensation, and some leaking, with long stalactites hanging from them.

Looking down again I found all eyes turned towards me, but I was conscious more of the mouths than anything, it seemed to be the mouths that saw me and judged me. The floor was carpeted with moving mouths, each with a rhythm all its own. Some champed quickly, shaking the loose flesh on the throat of the chewer like jelly. Others moved slowly like the beat of the heart, and these looked more friendly. One, all black with a black tongue, operated from the middle of a great black beard, which wagged and rippled. Some seemed to work sideways rather than up-and-down, some bore moustaches which writhed and rippled like bristly caterpillars, and there were toothless mouths which shut too far. But most of them seemed not to shut at all, and as I watched the rows of tongues deftly turning the balls of moist food, some clockwise and some anti-clockwise, I was reminded again of the action of a concrete-mixer. Then one by one the mouths lost interest in me and turned away to receive a sandwich or scrutinise a newspaper.

One of the mouthmen rose, walked on the stomachs and heads of his companions to the far wall and urinated against it. I realised then that this was not a canteen at all, but a toilet, and for the first time I noticed the rows of familiar small green cubicles. These had doors which did not come down to the ground, and beneath each door protruded feet, mostly in pairs but sometimes in threes and fours. A faded notice bore the words 'Your co-operation is requested in keeping this toilet clean and hygienic', under which someone had written in bold letters the word 'SHIT'. Through the smoke I could see only one man who was not eating, who stood motionless in a corner grasping an up-ended mop. He had the appearance of some kind of supervisor, and I thought that I would make my way towards him. I could not find a place to put my feet, however, and eventually stepped on a man's arm by mistake. I apologised at once, but he seemed not to notice and carried on reading a small grease-stained piece of newspaper which had printed on it the lower half of a naked female body and part of a crossword puzzle. I overbalanced slightly and trod on another man's leg, but he seemed not to notice either, so I stepped out smartly as a firewalker might, and reached the standing man in five strides, stepping on a stomach, a foot, a head, another head and a groin, in that order and without complaint.

Seeing the man at close quarters now I decided at once that he was the strangest looking man I had ever looked at. He was not tall. The top of his head was circular and completely flat, formed of the greasy cloth cap common to working men (of lower orders), and the distance between the peak of this and the bottom of his chin seemed to be about two inches. Sandwiched into this space was the thinnest and horizontally the widest mouth I have ever seen, and a generous ginger moustache. Nose and eyes seemed to be missing, or they may have been on top of his head under the cap. A black pipe stuck out of the mouth. (None of this disturbed me. Once upon a time, when I was fresh from school, my ideas of what a human being looked like were gained mostly from films and magazines and portraits of royalty, etc., and I believed, as most young people do, that almost all human faces conformed to a sort of standard pattern as do the faces of animals. I imagined that all human beings had two eyes, a nose in the centre of the face and a mouth at the bottom. I thought that the human face was always symmetrical like animal faces, and was usually at least pleasant to look at. But soon after entering the real world to earn a living I learnt that no ideal or normal face exists, that no two human faces are alike in the slightest, that their form and layout are so varied and often so incredibly ugly that they must outstrip even the most tormented imagination. I have seen men with pouches like sacks on one side of their faces, or eyes so far apart that they had to turn their heads to one side in order to see in front of them, like birds. One man who works near me has eyes on top of his head and has to draw his head so low into his chest in order to see in front of him that his arms seem to spring from the back of his skull like horns. I have seen dogs and cattle flee at the sight of him, but children never. When every face is freakish, then the freak is normal. All these people lead normal lives. Their mothers reared them gladly and other women marry them. We must all make do with these human faces, for there are no others.)

Suddenly this man said, without moving or taking his pipe from his mouth, the words, 'Sex again', and he said them in a way that a man who had eaten nothing but beans for seven years might say, on sitting down to a meal, 'Beans again'. I thought that my best plan would be to say something neutral like 'Good morning' in reply to this, but then he said, 'They can't seem to talk about anything else; but if the truth be known half of 'em couldn't manage a stand if you put it to 'em.' I asked who 'they' were, and in reply he waved an arm and kicked a nearby man on the shoulder. Then he did take his pipe from his mouth, and his head tipped up and came swooping up towards my ear. 'I could tell you things about these people,' he began in a barely audible croak, 'to make you throw up for a week.' It was like being spoken to by an old oyster. The mouth, the corners of which disappeared round each side of his head, opened no more than a fraction of an inch and snapped shut on the tails of the syllables as if it suspected the ginger moustache of intending to nip inside between words. 'I've seen things in here that no man should see.' At this the head drew back a little from my ear and seemed to be surveying my face for the satisfaction of seeing an astonished or unbelieving expression. But I saw no eyes anywhere. Again the oyster swooped in and offered, 'I've heard things to make my ears turn black in here.' I could see no ears either. 'Some come for a talk, some for a rest, or to eat their sandwiches like now.' Then he came so close I thought he might nip my ear by accident, and breathed, 'But most come to be alone.' He paused. 'Really?' I said. 'Never, never,' he went on, 'never anywhere else but in my little cubicles are they ever able to be alone. They move through day and night constantly in the presence of each other and wives and children, at work, in buses and trains, in bed, everywhere.' He paused, and looked quickly around as if afraid of being overheard. 'Did you know that even in prisons they have spyholes in the doors?' I said that I didn't. 'No!' he said. 'No, when they come in here, all breathless and grabbing at their braces-buttons, they come in to choose a cubicle and lock the door. To be alone, really alone.' He paused, cast an eyeless glance over his shoulder again and hissed '– or so they think.' Then a low moaning noise came through the lips, which might have been some kind of laugh, then, 'Not even a mirror to see 'em' – another moan – 'I could make yer skin crawl at some of the things. My toilet' he emphasised the 'my' – 'and I have to clean up afterwards and scrape the walls to get 'em off. But some use a hammer and chisel.' Again the moan. 'I could tell British Railways about "Improper Use of Chain". The things I find in the washbasins. You'd think the chaps would have more self-respect. Only yesterday, that cubicle' – he indicated a cubicle behind me – 'had to break in, chap hanging by his braces, tool in his hand.' I was shocked, and said that it must have been awful. 'It was,' he said. 'I broke the lock and had to put a new one on.'

He said nothing for some time and I began to feel slightly awkward. The noise of mastication continued, and reminded me that I had no sandwiches of my own. I did not particularly want to stay here, I was just wasting time. But I couldn't bring myself to say goodbye to this man and tread on all these people to face that lonely corridor again. I thought it unfriendly of me not to be more forthcoming, so, with a view to opening a serious conversation with my companion, I said to him, 'It is my belief that all things have a rational explanation.' Instantly the oyster swooped upwards to me and said, 'There's no women come in here, you know.' I had two reactions to this statement, but before I could choose which of them to put into words first he said, 'Like prisons and armies and primitive natives, just the same you know.' He came closer. 'When there's something nasty to do, like killing people or some barbarous ritual, or what they do here, they always send the women away, or lock 'em out. Women have got more sense, you see. They'd stop it.'

I was about to protest that one could not compare what went on in the jungles of Africa with a factory in England, in the twentieth century, when he asked me if I knew about the story of Jekyll and Hyde. I said I did, and he said that it was just like that with these men. I asked him to explain. 'Well, they've all got families, these chaps, wives and children, and they're like Jesus Christ in their own homes – their kids think they're marvellous and their wives slave for 'em.' He paused. 'You're a young chap. Your father work in a factory?' I replied that he did and worked in this factory, as it happened, though I'd never met him here. 'Well, there you are then!' he said, as if all should now be plain to me. 'He's all right, isn't he?' I answered that my father was as upright a man as ever I had met, and that I had never heard a bad word spoken of him by anyone. The oyster-mouth smiled as nearly as it was capable, and a hand patted me once or twice on the back. 'Of course not!' he said. 'You've never heard him swear at home, have you? I mean, not like they do here?' I said that I certainly had not, my father did not swear. 'And he doesn't bully you or your mother, or whistle at women in the street, or remark on their proportions? You've never known him show fear of anyone, or bow and scrape or toady up to people for a few bob, or speak disrespectfully of people, or spit, or cheat, or steal, or play nasty tricks on people just for the fun of it?' I said that I certainly had never known him to do any of these things, and that I didn't care for the tone of the conversation. He said loudly, 'Of course!' and slapped me hard on the back. 'It's the same with these chaps, their sons think the world of 'em. They go back there every night, good as gold, and if you met 'em in the street with their wives on a Sunday afternoon you wouldn't know 'em.' He paused. 'You say he works here?' I said he did. 'You never see him here, though?' 'No, not in sixteen years,' I said. He was thoughtful for a few seconds, and then, after glancing to left and to right and over his shoulder a ridiculous number of times, he came unbelievably close to my ear and hissed, 'Do you think you'd recognise him?' after which he drew back to observe my reaction.

I was about to protest to him when suddenly everyone in the room climbed to their feet and began to file out of the door. When both doors were open I could hear the wailing of a siren out in the corridor. The doors of all the cubicles swung open and large numbers of men walked out, fastening or hitching up their trousers and putting on their overalls. They all filed out of the door and when the last one had gone I looked round to find that my oyster friend had also disappeared, and that I was alone. The floor was littered with crumpled paper bags and bits of damp newspaper. I could hear the buzz of flies above me, and the drip of water, and other noises of water: water in tanks, water hissing, water shaking and banging the pipes about as if it were alive, snarling in a basin where someone had left a tap on, water creeping, running, soaking, falling, rising in vapour, drowning spiders, feeding mosses, rusting iron, rotting the doorposts of the cubicles, sustaining the thirsty flies. I shivered and thought it best to go. Not before making use of a WC, however. I walked towards one of the green doors and was about to push it open when I remembered the hanging business, and tried to decide which cubicle the old man had indicated, for I didn't like the idea of sitting where a man had just hung himself. The rope might still be there, or something equally nasty. I went to the next cubicle and tried to discover from the outside if the lock had recently been replaced, and as there were no signs of this I made as if to push the door, but then stopped and went back to the other one. This looked exactly the same as the other so I went back again to see the first, but I didn't like the look of that this time. I noticed a puddle of water under the door, so I went back to the other, which also seemed to have water on the floor. In despair I walked three or four paces to my right, pushed open the nearest cubicle door and was confronted, not by a lavatory basin and cistern, but by a woman sitting on a chair with a telephone by her side.

I was surprised and stood there stupidly for a second. I was about to apologise when she asked me to step inside and close the door. She said it so firmly that I did so at once. Then she said, 'Well, bolt it, stupid.' 'Bolt it?' I said. 'Well, you wouldn't go into a lavatory and not bolt the door, would you?' she said impatiently. I bolted it. I was completely at a loss for something to say. I must go out, but I had just locked myself in. When I had first opened the door I had thought that this was an office of some kind, but looking at the walls now I saw that it must have been a lavatory until quite recently, for they were generously covered with the popular art and literature characteristic of such places. There were the neat little anecdotes carefully written, the single words scrawled in bold vehement letters, the careful anatomical drawings, meticulous in parts but with the extremities tailing off as the artist became impatient with his lack of skill. There were the promises and appointments, ending in 'Don't be late', or 'Wear a red buttonhole', and the sad little advertisements; also the brisker, more precise ones giving measurements and curious or mysterious specifications and conditions of contract. Here were all the sorrows, dreams and improvisations of my fellow workers, expressed as the oysterman said, in solitude and anonymity.

The woman's voice had been rasping and unattractive and her appearance was strange. She was dressed only in a thick petticoat and a pair of red combinations which came down to her knees. She was very thin, and the petticoat straps went over her shoulders in a series of sharp angles. She looked about thirty, perhaps more, her eyes tired, and shadowed without any artificial aid. A clump of greenish hair was harassed by a strange collection of pins, curlers and artificial flowers, and held high on her head by bands of ribbon, revealing a thin but graceful neck. Her limbs were thin and hairy. Only the lips and mouth were generous, disturbingly so, so that half her head seemed covered in lipstick. The mouth was so wide that I was convinced she must be the oysterman's daughter, and decided to go. 'I think that I must have come in here by mistake,' I said, 'for there must be a rational explanation.' She said that she thought that there probably wasn't at all, and that after all there never was, but here I was and she would like to help me if it was at all possible. 'Help me?' I said. 'But surely there's a problem I can help you with?' she said. 'Wouldn't you like to let me try?' I said awkwardly, 'You – you help people with their problems?' 'With their most distressing and personal problems,' she replied. I thought for a moment. Perhaps indeed she could help me, or at least tell me where to go and whom to find to answer this question of mine. There was the telephone. She was probably in touch with all the most important people in the whole factory, or at least with those in this department. 'Are you in touch with all the important people in this department?' I asked, indicating the telephone. 'I am in touch with all the important people in the whole factory,' she said. Yes, obviously she was the right person to ask.

'I'm sure you can help me,' I said. 'You see, I seem to have been nothing but a burden to my wife recently, even our most casual contacts and most natural relations have become quite difficult.' 'You needn't tell me any more, I understand perfectly,' she said. 'Of course I can help you.' I was about to say that I had hardly begun, when she said that she hoped I didn't mind standing up as there wasn't room to lie on the floor. I replied that I was quite happy to stand up, and did not at all want to lie on the floor. 'You would prefer to stand up?' she said. 'No, I would prefer to sit on a chair,' I said, but since there was only one here I was sure that she would think it improper of me to sit down. She replied that she didn't think it at all improper, that surely one chair was enough and that many people preferred to sit rather than lie down. I said that surely most people preferred different positions at different times of the day, but that in this case it was a matter of propriety. 'If I were with a man it would be different,' I said. 'It would be quite normal for me to sit down if I were with a man. It wouldn't make much difference who sat on the chair, he or I.' She said yes, she supposed that must be so, and stood up and insisted that I sit on the chair. 'But don't you mind?' I asked. 'I don't mind at all,' she replied. 'I really don't. You can hang from the wall by your feet if you like, though it might be very difficult like that. Some of them like to stand on their heads in the corner or swing from the doorframe. If they like it better that way I always try not to discourage them, if it's physically possible for me to do anything with them like that, of course.'

I sat on the chair and she undressed very suddenly. Her belly was flat and covered in little scars. She saw me looking at them and said, 'You get those when you're pregnant,' and straightaway leapt on to me and gripped me with her legs, and bounced about so that her breasts made flopping noises. I was taken by surprise, but suddenly felt an urge to make the most of the situation whatever its explanation might be. I asked her to get off again and stood up, lowered my trousers and sat down again, and she remounted. But if my mind was willing my flesh seemed not to be, and all her jiggling about and all my concentration had no effect. After a while I apologised, but she said not to worry, that this often happened, and if I would keep quite still and stare into her eyes all would be well. I did this for what seemed an age, and then suddenly I did feel a faint stirring, and told her so, whereupon the telephone rang and she had to go and answer it. She whispered down it, replaced it and remounted me. 'The Manager,' she said, 'I told him that you were here.'

I said that I thought we'd have to start again. She expressed annoyance, but we engaged eyes and after ten minutes or so there was a faint stirring again, and when I told her she whistled through her teeth like a snake charmer and the stirring increased. I clenched my teeth and fists. 'I'm ready, then,' I said, and she started to jump about again and clasped me tighter with her legs so that her hip-bones dug into me painfully. But if I was now ready, she did not seem to be, or else she had a very peculiar anatomy, and twist and turn as I might I could not find her. It occurred to me then what a hideous joke of nature it is that in this, surely the trickiest mechanical operation in the whole natural world, we are denied the use of our eyes. I wondered how it was that insects and other low creatures, who could have little idea in advance of what it was they were trying to do, and moreover had no hands, could ever successfully copulate. But obviously they did, and here was I incapable of doing what the meanest cockroach could do with ease. We struggled and strained together, her heels digging into my buttocks. I rose from the chair with her clinging to me, grasped her hips firmly in my hands and moved them about systematically. I sweated and gasped, she twisted this way and that and groaned and broke the spell like a hammer.

Overcome with shame and frustration I threw her down, grabbed at my trousers, unbolted the door and rushed out. I was hardly through the door when a great bearded man with hair spilling and tumbling out of his open shirtfront and tattoos all over his forearms rushed past me into the cubicle and slammed the door. A great crowd of such men had gathered in the main room, some of them eight feet tall with chests like bass drums, some bare to the waist with the arms of their overalls tied round their waists, parading their chests around and covered in tattoos or hair or both. Others had no trousers, and leapt nimbly about sporting huge erections like tree-trunks, chasing each other with them and banging them together like clubs so that the ground shook. Yet others were wrestling naked with deep grunts and gasps, piled in struggling heaps of three and four with their strapping limbs locked in unbelievable holds. One man, naked save for a great erection wrapped in newspaper, stood twisting and stroking his ginger moustachios while a man behind him skipped up and down thumping him in the back with terrible blows. There were some who bounced around like athletes warming up before a major trial of strength and endurance, thumping their chests and slapping their thighs, jerking and twisting in ferocious and terrible exercises, hissing through their teeth like steam engines. And all were waiting, waiting to go through that door, and above the noise of grunting and thumping I could hear a noise as if every cistern in the lavatory were boiling and bursting and flushing and flooding over into all the gutters of all the streets of England, and I clutched my trousers about me and ran from that place through the double doors and into the corridor and away.

chapter two

I found myself walking through a part of the factory where the painters had just been, for everything which could be painted was painted either dark green, grey or rough surfaced aluminium silver, and the usual layer of dust and dirty grease had not yet obliterated these colours. Once, years ago, we had a whole lot of men in white coats come swarming about the factory, asking us questions about colours, what colours we painted our bedrooms, what did we think of this and that colour and having the machines and the walls painted all sorts of colours. In our department we had to have yellow-green walls with pink woodwork, and the machines were painted orange with light blue patches and all moving parts bright scarlet. Then they watched us, hiding behind doors and inside cupboards with notebooks, scribbling away. We always knew where they were because they all smoked pipes with expensive tobacco and you could smell them a mile away. It was the same all over the factory, I was told – not the colours, the colours were always different, the men in white coats, I mean. Some carried big watches on chains and others had cameras and binoculars. Of course, knowing that we were being watched and because it was so nice to feel that someone was taking an interest in us, we all worked harder, everyone in the factory. After a few weeks they all disappeared and we went back to the old green, grey and aluminium paint after a very short time, which of course disappeared under the dirt very soon.

But I had heard tell of a band of painters who roamed the factory, painting as they went. We had never seen them up at my department in fifteen years and there was, we knew, a great deal of factory to paint; but there was no doubt that the sons or grandsons of these men would eventually reach us – we were always quite certain of that. Every springtime we would hear rumours that the painters were coming: someone had smelt paint in the air, or seen a green or silver footprint in a gangway, or long ladders poking up in the distance above the machinery. Then we would all become very excited and rush round scraping off the grease and scrubbing and cleaning in preparation for them, and someone would say, 'They expect free beer, you know,' and we would all bring in bottles of beer and put them away in a cupboard in readiness. But spring would turn to summer and summer to autumn and no painters – so that in the end we would drink the beer little by little and try to forget about them. The springcleans were very useful, mind. Sometimes we would find whole machines under the dirt which everyone had forgotten about, and dig them out and shine them up and start using them again. Once we dug up a skeleton, but we never found out whose it was.

Now, here I was, walking through a forest of newly painted machines. When I get back to the slotters, I said to myself, I shall tell them that I have seen this, and that will be very encouraging for everybody. Perhaps I should speak to a painter now, I thought, while I was here, and ask him if he knew when they might get to us, or even ask him to try to persuade his comrades to make a special visit. I could promise him very special beer, or more than usual of it, or perhaps whisky and soda instead. At any rate there could be no harm in asking, so I stepped out more briskly and looked around me as I went.

It was rather dark here, however, and the machines were all very tall and close together so that I couldn't see far in any direction other than directly ahead of me. Above me, in the roof, were the usual expanses of glass, made up, as factory windows always seem to be, of odd lengths and bits of all kinds of glass. There are pieces of pimply glass, and sometimes green glass with those lumps in like the bottoms of bottles, and often glass with wire netting embedded in it. I have seen knobbly bathroom door glass and glass with thick ribs running across it, and even pieces of etched glass which came from some old public house which the factory had supplanted. But all of this one was stained, as factory windows often are, with broad parallel streaks of brown and black where dirt had been carried down the glass year after year from some old chimney or piece of rusty metal, and with expanses of translucent yellow and green where lichens had grown, spreading across the panes from the cracks and crevices, feeding on the older dirt. Yes, we have our stained-glass windows too, filtering the raw light of the outside to fit the business within. Often when I got home in the evenings I would say to my wife, 'What has the weather been like for you today?' and she might tell me that the sun had shone brilliantly all day, or that there had been a thunderstorm at 3 o'clock with many flashes of lightning and thunder, but I would know nothing of it, the machinery would have drowned the thunder as well. The weather in a factory is always the same, dull, warm and dry. In order to make accurate work possible at any time when the general lighting is switched off – which is, of course, most of the day – each machine has its own small lamp, a sad little thing in a dirty tin reflector, adjustable but always too floppy, so that it never stays where you put it. These lamps shine out like little camp fires in all the gloom, lighting up perhaps just the side of a man's face, or his hand on a wheel. I have often noticed how a machine without its lamp lit has a strange, dead look about it as if it were only a grey wooden imitation of a machine, not really capable of working at all, and if a man is with it he will look blue or grey like a corpse.

The eyes didn't bother me now and there were fewer of them. I thought of my wife at home, and looked up at a clock. I have heard that in prisons they have no clocks because time is only a burden. In a factory, however, time is like gold, every gramme of it is weighed and then the floor-sweepings too, and factories bulge with clocks. There are two or three massive ones hung high up in every department, and scores of little ones all over the partitions or any other flat vertical surfaces. They peep through the windows of the offices and stand in corners where you can't see them looking at you. On the clocking-in machines are faceless clocks which just show you three figures through a little glass window. All these are controlled, so I gather, by a little 'master clock' which is kept in the manager's office, which doesn't look like a clock at all and doesn't even tell you the time. It tells all the clocks the time, and in a characteristically managerial sort of way, because factory clocks don't amble along in that friendly way of old clocks or clocks with second hands taking you steadily along from one minute to the next. Factory clocks jump. One minute it's 3.53 exactly, and then, just as you've begun to suspect that all the clocks have stopped, it's suddenly 3.54 by every single one of them, without so much as a second's warning, take it or leave it. 'And 3.54,' they seem to say, 'it will jolly well stay until it's time to be 3.55, and if you want to know if we're halfway yet you should mind your own business and get on with your work.' At the moment it was 11.13, and I couldn't be bothered to wait to find out which end of it.

My wife, I thought, would probably be in the kitchen, doing one kind of cleaning or another and finding the children difficult. When I was younger I disliked leaving the house all day to go to work, but whenever I'm at home now I realise what a good thing it is that I'm out of her way on most days. I get so bored, and we get on each other's nerves.

I'm usually glad to be back at work on a Monday. Without a lot of money it's impossible to amuse yourself when you have any leisure. That's why most men work all the overtime they can get. It's bad for the children to have a father mooning about the house. Now if we had a car or two, and could pop down to the seaside and do some sailing, that would be different. But for a working man it's his duty to keep out of the way as much as possible, and try to earn a bit more money. That's what my father told me when I left school. 'What's the use of your studies,' he'd say, 'if you spend half your time sitting about. Get a good job, earn some money. Work hard all your life, and if you're careful you'll have enough money to enjoy your retirement.' I've always respected my father. He could have retired years ago, but still he goes on working and saving, twelve hours a day, seven days a week. A very hardworking and prudent man is my father.

There were no painters to be seen, and then it occurred to me that the smell of the new paint wasn't really very strong. I touched a vertical girder, splendid with gleaming grey paint. It was quite dry and hard. I rubbed my finger across it and examined the finger closely. There was already a film of dust on the girder. But I would catch up with them soon, I was sure.

A few yards in front of me a labourer emerged from between the piles of components carrying a heavy casting, crossed the gangway and disappeared amongst the components on the other side. As I drew level with the spot he emerged empty handed, brushing his hands together as one who has done a good job and is glad to be finished. He was short and stocky, with ginger hair, ginger freckles and a mouth which hung open in an empty sort of way. I shouted to him above the noise of the machinery, 'Good morning, have you seen any painters about here anywhere?' He looked surprised and stopped brushing his hands. He glanced quickly behind him as if to see if I was speaking to someone else; then he didn't seem to know what to do with his hands, and stared at them as if they'd only just grown. 'Painters,' I shouted, in case he hadn't heard above the din. 'Mainers,' he said through his nose vacantly. I prodded the freshly painted surface of a cupboard. He shrugged his shoulders.

Just then another man appeared carrying a large casting exactly like the other one, also the man himself was so like the labourer to whom I was already speaking that I thought they must be brothers. As he staggered across the gangway with little hopping steps the pair exchanged glances and looked at me, then at each other again and then again at me, as if there was something strange about me. But in a factory, where a man might see the same few faces every day for about twenty years, all strangers are strange. The second man disappeared to the right. There was a crash and a few seconds later he reappeared, flexing his shoulders and arms with relief. 'Mainers,' said his friend, pointing to the cupboard. The newcomer strode over to the cupboard at once and applied his finger to it. No 1 lost interest then, and disappeared across the gangway while No 2 took out a notebook from his trouser pocket and began to thumb through it. His friend reappeared carrying another casting just like the others, in fact, it looked as if he was taking back the casting which his companion had just carried across. No 2 looked up from his notebook and fired a question at him which I did not hear, and he tried to shrug his shoulders, which was impossible, so he shrugged his eyebrows instead, then carried on across the gangway and disappeared between two tall piles of machine parts.

'They were here two weeks ago,' said No 2, looking closely at the book. The other labourer reappeared, puffing and blowing, whereupon No 2 apologised, put away his notebook and hurried off through the gap from which his friend had just emerged. No 1 fixed me with his eye and came very close, as if about to tell me something rather confidential. He looked behind him quickly, then said out of the corner of his mouth, 'Ar hint nay ver-rere hoo wits-uno.' I thanked him and said that the other man had already told me this, which made him stare at me in amazement. No 2 staggered across the gangway again with the casting. It must be the same casting, I thought, though I knew that there were probably two thousand identical castings somewhere about. They never carried them the same way twice running; No 1 always carried them to the right and No 2 always to the left.

They changed places again, No 2 slightly breathless but with his book already in his hand. 'Today,' he said, 'and all this week they will be working in the heat-treatment shops.' I thanked him, as the casting crossed the gangway again from left to right. Halfway across the man had a coughing fit and struggled to hold his load, balancing it first on one knee and then on the other until he had recovered. Then he hurried on, wheezing and spitting, to get rid of the thing as soon as possible. 'Where is that?' I said. 'Oh, a long way from here,' he replied, waving an arm in no particular direction. 'I could tell you, but you'd only get lost.' 'I'm lost already,' I replied. 'Where do you want to go?' he asked, and slipped away as his friend joined us, still coughing and spitting. The man seemed to know a good deal about the factory, I thought. I felt silly at not having made some enquiries before setting out this morning – and yet there had been no-one to ask in the slotting section. Soon I must tell someone all about it, and ask advice, but I didn't relish putting myself into the hands of a labourer. He crossed the gangway again from right to left, long strings standing out on his arms. He carried the object with his arms straight, so that it rested on his knees, forcing him to shuffle forward by moving his legs only from the knees downwards, while his head wagged about from side to side to keep him balanced. But he seemed an intelligent man; why he should be a labourer I could not think, much less why he should devote himself to dragging a single casting backwards and forwards, if that was what he was doing. As he made his way between the piles I felt an impulse to run over and mark a chalk across the casting. But it was none of my business. The other man, who stood watching me with his arms hanging down like a gibbon, came close again and glanced over his shoulder several times in preparation for speaking. (Lower orders always do this. It is a deeply rooted habit of making sure that the foreman isn't watching or someone listening who shouldn't be.) 'Nayr ineet-hreetmen orni hwint,' he said. 'I know,' I said, 'your friend told me.' Again he looked absolutely amazed, as if he thought I was some kind of magician.

No 2 joined us again, and No 1 slouched off towards the gap through which his friend had just carried his burden. 'I wonder if you could help me,' I began. 'I have a very worrying problem – it might not seem very worrying or very important to you, but to me it is absolutely vital that I should find the answer.' 'Go on,' he said. 'To be quite frank, I feel rather embarrassed at telling you: I have never actually spoken to anyone about it before.' No 1 emerged with the casting, clutching it very awkwardly and pulling a dreadful face. I went on, 'I work in the slotting section' – No 2 nodded as if he knew exactly where that was, or at least how to find out from his little book – 'and I have worked on one particular kind of component for the past twenty years, a pulley, 436/3741/G.' No 2 pulled a face. 'I have often wondered,' I went on, 'what happened to these pulleys' – there was a loud crash: No 1 had arrived – 'and recently the question obsessed me beyond all reason.' No 2 excused himself and his companion rejoined me, his face red and running with sweat. He stood and eyed me very warily, picking his nose while trying to pretend he wasn't, while No 2 staggered back across the corridor emitting a great exploding gasp at each step.

When he had finished and the two men had changed places again, I continued, 'I think that life will have no meaning for me until I have found out exactly where my particular effort fits in, what service it performs, who eventually uses it, for what purposes. You probably think I'm a sentimental old fool,' I said, suddenly feeling embarrassed. He pulled a face which might have meant that he did or that he didn't. Out of the corner of my eye I saw the casting crossing the gangway again. It must be the same one, I thought. 'But I can assure you that it was only after great suffering and despair that I was driven to make this journey.' The crash again, and the ground shook. No 1 staggered across, his chest heaving, and doubled up with his hands on his knees as No 2 again took his leave. He returned with the notebook already open in his hands. Gasping for breath he prodded it and said, 'You must go to the General Parts Stores, they know all about everything there. They know what everything is used for, they have to.' He then gave me, between sessions of carrying, long detailed instructions of how to get to the General Parts Stores. He drew diagrams in chalk on the floor, which astounded his companion more and more each time he rejoined us, until I was sure that he thought I was the devil at least. When eventually I left them, thanking them very sincerely, my head was buzzing with the weight of it all. Never mind, I thought. I shall go as far as I can and then ask someone else. At least I had a destination now.

I walked on, and presently noticed that there were many things which were quite different in this part of the factory. There were no eyes at all now. The components were all larger than those I was familiar with, and there seemed to me to be a ridiculous abundance of them. In our department the parts come in boxes or large skips, and we unload them from one container into another as we work so that they don't clutter up the floor. But here they were all on the floor, most of them stacked in tall columns too high to see over and too close together for a man to pass between. Some of the larger, flatter castings stood in columns as high as four men, and looked quite dangerous. As I walked between these stacks I noticed how it was that each different kind of component formed columns which had a distinct character, the various repeated shapes and forms of the component creating a vertical pattern which was unlike that created by any other component. Often a particular kind of casting, because of its unsymmetrical or awkward shape, had to be stacked with a slight spiral in order that the column should stand securely. One component, which had three long arms radiating from its centre, formed stacks which looked like giant spinal columns from some old dinosaur. But mostly they reminded me of pictures I had seen of the trunks of palm trees, or bare Brussels sprout stalks, or fantastic plants from the coal age, all grey and fossilised. Apart from my gangway, these columns monopolised all the available floor-space, and the place looked like a jungle or a glass-house in Kew Gardens, where human beings might have to scramble around the roots of an infinite variety of enormous plants which scratched and caught at the clothing.

But very strange were the men. Watching a group of them through a gap in the stacks, each one at his machine, I was reminded more than anything of ballet dancers on television. I thought then that if they had the time they could have looked quite graceful – yes, that was it, they looked like ballet dancers speeded up on a film, speeded up so that they looked ridiculous and undignified, or a bit insane. Each one repeated the pattern of his actions strictly and accurately, with not a finger or a hair moving unnecessarily. They moved quickly but not quite jerkily, with each movement blended into the next, the momentum of each movement carried over into the next, so that the minimum of effort was wasted in braking or reversing any part of the body. They displayed not so much ambidexterity as polydexterity, so that while one hand was occupied in lifting or shifting the component and the other perhaps in preparing a clamp to receive it, a foot might be used to raise or lower the table, or the nose might press a start or stop button. I could see one man who was moving his eyes independently of each other, keeping one on the machine while using the other in preparation for the next component. Now I saw one who was, without pausing in his work, rolling a cigarette behind his back while deftly tightening a nut with a spanner held between his teeth. I could see another man unwrapping his lunch-packet with his knees while his hands paused not at all in their work. There was never any respite, these men did not stop for a second the whole time I watched. Every pause, while the machine was cutting, or its tables travelling from one position to another, was used to prepare the next component or to move it to a better position ready for its turn. The patterns were repeated again and again, the hands falling in exactly the same place at exactly the same time, the feet one, two, turn, together as before. Each man's cycle of movements lasted a different length of time, so that the rhythms of the group interacted with each other to form an infinitely changing pattern of movement. The machines leapt and tumbled under the fingers of the men as if they had come alive, and the men worked as if they had become machines, and I felt as if I were watching one of those mechanical peepshow affairs I'd seen in fairgrounds, and I also remembered a fantastic clock I once saw in the Horniman Museum one rainy day which marked the hours with a full parade of the disciples simultaneously with the birth, death, resurrection and ascension. But whatever possessed these men that they should work like this, I wondered?

One man was operating what I knew to be a vertical mill, of giant proportions. It towered above him, and its slotted table stretched out to left and to right far enough to lay out two corpses end to end on the cold ground iron, the grooves there ready to catch the blood in. In front of the table his hands danced on the controls, so that the roaring cutter rose and fell and swerved around the contours of the component, while the iron turned to water before it. The howling cutter ran over the casting like a mouse, it was impossible to believe that it had not eyes and ears and a quick mind of its own. Then in an instant it had leapt off into the air, and the jig was open, and the cycle of the man's dance had begun again. Where did the man end and the machine begin, I wondered? Is not a musical instrument in the hands of a great player as much a part of him as his vocal chords and tongue and mouth? Ask a man how he operates his vocal chords, and he will say, 'I speak, what else can I tell you?' Similarly, another man might say, 'I play,' and this one would shrug and say, 'I mill.'

Suddenly I was aware of a man standing beside me, who said, guessing my thoughts, 'We are corpses, are we not? Dancing corpses. We dance and they throw coins at us. At the end of the week we pick them up and go off and pay someone to feed us, and someone else to play football for us, and someone else to make up the road outside our house, and someone else to take away our garbage. We delegate to someone else the task of keeping order in our own street, pay men we never see to make us a television set and men we never meet to entertain us by it. Our chairs, cutlery, crockery, coal, coats, clocks, cycles and cigarettes, our whole houses, are made for us by other people, and so there is nothing left to us but our corpses.'

'I am from another part of the factory,' I said, 'and have never in my life seen men work like this. Surely there must be a rational explanation.' He chuckled over my shoulder. 'There is an explanation. We are working piecework.' I said that I had heard of this system, but had never had any experience of it. 'It's easy to see that,' he said, 'by the way

you stand and breathe and talk. A man can only die once.'
'But surely,' I said, 'you live. You go home, you kiss your
wives, sit in armchairs and play with your children like
anyone else, and you must earn more money than most. You
look as if you each do the work of three men.' 'We do!' he
ejaculated. 'By God, we do! But we aren't paid the wages of
three men.' I expressed surprise. 'There is the trickery of it,'
he said. 'If we work three times as hard as a man may
reasonably be expected to work, and complete three times as
many operations in the given time, we earn what is known as
treble time.' I nodded. 'But treble time is not treble pay, my
friend, it is a rate of pay about twenty per cent higher than
normal pay. That is normal practice in any factory. It is what
the management calls "sharing the profits of higher output".
They throw down a few extra shillings, and we go scrapping
and scrabbling for them like dogs in the gutter. And so if a
corpse with a wife and children is to keep body and soul
together it must dance till all hours, and no time for kissing
or playing with them.' 'But you must go home at some time
and live and make love and dig the garden,' I protested. He
sniggered, 'Oh, yes, we go home sometimes. But have you
ever seen us go? At the end of the week we go dancing and
skipping down the corridor trying to put our coats on while
our hands and feet carry on with the routine, pulling the
levers and turning the wheels all the way home on the bus so
that people stare, and cross over to the other side of the road
when they see us coming along. We go home, but we can't
keep still for five minutes in an armchair, and our kids won't
come near us for fear we'll pull their arms and legs and screw
their noses off, and a meal's no pleasure if you can't sit at a
table or get a cup of tea to your mouth without spilling it all
down you. Even the wife's got fed up with being treated like
a broaching machine, so we sleep separately now and I
always wake in the middle of the night shouting "Switch the
bloody thing off at the main", and all the blankets on the

floor and the bed half taken to pieces. Home life? Dancing corpses, I tell you.' For the first time I looked at him, and saw that he hopped and twitched about, and every so often swung round half a circle and back again with his arms positioned as if holding something.

He cocked an ear suddenly, and in the distance I could hear a roaring noise, not like the wind but like some animal, and coming closer. A coloured labourer ran past us gibbering, then a man driving a stacker-truck at a great rate who shouted something to us as he passed, warning us about something, but I couldn't quite make out what. My friend laughed, picked up a piece of nothing and said, 'Foreman'. The roaring was closer now, and I could hear that it was composed mostly of threats, curses and insults uttered in a continuous stream. 'Not your foreman?' I said. He nodded, winding an invisible handle and squinting. A bunch of labourers rushed past, some dragging trolleys, some trundling wheelbarrows or pushing small trucks, all making a fearful noise of clattering and jabbering. Then the man who was roaring came into view, striding out and flailing his arms about. He had the appearance of some legendary circus ringmaster. The centre of his body seemed to be his neck, which was so great that I was struck with the thought that here was a man who could put his shirt on without undoing the collar. But then I saw his eyebrows, and his nose – no, his collar would catch on that for sure, and the moustache, wild and spiky and the size of a bale of hay. Beneath that the mouth which was giving rise to all this commotion, open so wide and working so hard. I was afraid he might come sliding up out of his own gullet and turn inside out with rage. His hair was shining black and curly and writhed about on his head like a basket of eels. He was close to us now, roaring, and walking with a great humping limp. With every other step he heaved his shoulders up with the effort of lifting his leg, and now it seemed that every time he did so he heaved up the whole workshop around him, all the machines and all the men a foot in the air, and dropped us all with a crash while he swung his good leg forward. Up we went again, and the men at the machines looked around in terror as they worked, and then worked harder.

I glanced at my friend. He was grinning in an unpleasant sort of way as he manipulated his invisible machine. I suddenly realised that the full heat of the foreman's mouth was directed at us, and the meaty hands were being flung in our direction. My companion stopped his machine and reached over to another real one to pick up a very real and solid wrench. The foreman was coming towards us roaring and shrugging his way through the heaps of components like a gorilla in a jungle. My companion moved to meet him, shouting something very insulting and waving his wrench. The roaring man came on, shouting something about my friend having no respect for authority, which he answered by jumping forward and swinging the wrench into the side of the foreman's head with a crash. Any other man would have dropped unconscious on the spot, but this one displayed neither surprise nor pain, but continued bellowing and snatched up a large spanner from a nearby machine. They struck out at each other together then, and the wrench whacked into the porcine neck while the spanner missed its mark completely and whizzed back for another try, as the roaring curses became even louder. This time the irons met in the air with a crash, and to my relief the wrench broke and the spanner flew from the foreman's hand, for I was sure that either blow might easily have killed one of the men; but then they closed in to wrestle, the foreman raving and ranting about intending to have his authority respected and what obscene and humiliating punishments lay in store for my friend, whom he considered to be very inferior and dishonest, and so on; my friend replied with his boot, and the foreman crashed into a column of large hollow castings which toppled and fell like gongs between them. But the moustache reared up in an instant, and the men went reeling together into another column, and another, so that the air was full of falling components and the ringing of iron and the roaring of the foreman. Castings rolled and bounced all over the floor. The men working at the machines never looked round, but they seemed to be wrestling with their machines as they worked as if trying to influence the fight behind them. Then suddenly the foreman seemed to lose interest and went humping off down the corridor still raging about his authority, but with his attention on some poor coloured labourer further down the bay who, I think, had been shouting encouragement to my friend above the din, and they both disappeared, only the bellowing of the foreman rising from time to time above the noise of the machinery.

When the other pugilist returned to my side I asked him where I could find the General Parts Stores, for time was running on. The man looked puzzled. 'I've never heard of a General Parts Stores. Tool Stores, yes. We go there for our cutters. There's the Castings Stores, and the Components Waiting Stores.' 'It's a place where all the finished parts in the factory are stored awaiting assembly,' I said, 'or so I was told.' 'Never heard of it,' he said. 'Who told you?' 'Labourer.' 'Oh, that would account for it. They know everything, these labourer chaps. They have to. They know every component by sight, what machine it's due to go to and then where it has to be taken after that. Very often when they bring a job along I ask them what's to be done to it, just to refresh my memory. And they reel off all the dimensions and tolerances and settings, feeds, spindle speed and cutter size for that particular batch, without so much as looking in a notebook. And then maybe they get a crate in and half a dozen others out, where you and I wouldn't be able to turn round or know where to start. Like that game where you have to get a piece from one side of the board to another by shifting all the other pieces around, with only one vacant square all the time. They do it as easy as spitting, by algebra, one chap told me. You have to have a head on a job like that. They take five years to become fully trained, and have to pass exams. They have to know the whole factory inside out, from the foundry to the sales office. I wouldn't like to take on all that responsibility myself, what with the musclework as well you have to be an all-round superman. The cream of the factory, those labourers.'

I wished him a good morning and hurried on. I walked for what seemed miles through the dimness and din. I happened to notice that the machines around me were now almost all lathes, but such lathes as I'd never seen before. I'd always thought a lathe an altogether more friendly kind of machine. For all sorts of reasons. For one thing lots of men have a small lathe in their garden shed. You couldn't imagine anyone having a vertical mill or a surface grinder in his shed. It wouldn't be any use either, whereas a lathe – you can do anything with a lathe, make bowls and chairlegs and decorative brass-knobs, pokers, handles for anything. The list is endless.

But the lathes around me here weren't like that at all. To begin with, they were so large they were unnatural. A man with all his arms and legs spread out couldn't have covered one of the faceplates, and some of the beds were so long that the operator sat in a travelling chair which took him from one end of the machine to the other with the toolpost. Then there was the speed of them. There were no cutters, but the components were all whirling so fast that they looked almost as dangerous as cutters, and each operator worked in a private gale, hair dishevelled and clothing flapping. Instead of one little cutting tool the machines bristled with them, peeping out of the tool-holders in all sorts of places where I'd never seen them before, where they might catch anyone passing. Instead of one tool at the front, mounted on a single crosslide and controlled by one handle, there were dozens of toolbits in front of the operator mounted on at least half-a-dozen slides, and handles and wheels everywhere. There were toolposts approaching from behind the component sliding towards the operator, and others which came in from above and below at various angles. The tail stocks of these lathes were not the simple things I was familiar with: small affairs easily slid along the bed by hand, made to carry a small chuck, or a single drill, or a centrebit to steady the free end of the turning component; these tailstocks were huge saddle-like constructions which sat astride the bed and covered it down to the floor, obviously power-operated, surmounted by rotating turrets which bristled with multiple tool-bits and thread-chasers and whacking drills as thick as my wrist. No dignity here. I hurried on and came to a junction in the gangway.

Directly in front of me was the biggest machine I had ever seen. I judged from the noise it made and from the great stream of white sparks which hosed out from one side of it that it was a surface-grinder, but what a surface-grinder. You could have ground the walls of a house on it. The grinding wheel, which I calculated must have been as big as a large cartwheel, was completely hidden from view under a metal cowl that was the shape and size of a small oasthouse, the inside of which became by turns as bright as looking at the sun and black as midnight.

I must ask which way to the General Parts Stores, but the operator of this grinder was out of sight, somewhere on the other side with the controls. I started to walk round the machine, and was accompanied all down one side by the table, moving only slightly faster than I walked. By the time I had walked across the end, however, it was under the cowl again, flashing and crashing like a great rocket straining to take off. I tried to keep my eyes away from it, but the cowl was now in front of me. When the last casting had gone through and my eyes had cleared, I was standing at the base of the cowl, and found myself looking at a formidable control panel with coloured lights, and a large, scaly pig. The pig glanced at me briefly and continued winding a wheel. The wheel had a handle on it, but the pig wound it by putting its nose between two of the four spokes of the wheel and twiddling expertly and very quickly. The pig brought the wheel to a halt, gave it a last nudge or two, withdrew its nose and glanced up at the dials and lights. Evidently satisfied, it took a short, knobbed lever carefully in its mouth and pushed it to the right. I perceived that the table was now returning. The pig ambled off past me with a sniff and a snort. I caught sight of the operator of the next machine along, who was human and looking in my direction, so I waved and walked towards him. I was met halfway by the great table, its cargo of castings smoking slightly and glinting from ground surfaces as it passed me.

As I approached the next machine I saw that this was a powerful press, such as is used to punch or press out shapes from flat plates of soft steel. Its heavy bedplate, cut across with deep grooves for clamping, was straddled by four shining steel pillars as thick as a man's thigh, which supported the great ram, together with a flywheel like a millstone and various devices for stopping and starting the ram. Clamped to the bedplate was the large piece of metal which forms what is in effect the teeth of the press, if the bed may be looked on as the lower jaw and the ram as the upper. The raw metal was being fed through this now, and every few seconds there was a loud click and the ram dropped as if struck from above by some gigantic hammer, and returned. Each time it did so the ground shook, but the machine was not as noisy as most. The man, who continued to work the machine and feed the metal through in a long strip, greeted me very cheerfully. He wore a black and red striped football jersey, and overalls with the top part rolled down to his waist, the arms tied round his middle like a belt. His face was all bulbous, his skin very greasy, and his fat lips formed a giant smile. 'Good morning,' I said. 'I was very surprised to see a pig in charge of a surface-grinder.' The man laughed, a great generous bubbling laugh like a slap on the back. 'Yes, he's a pig all right! Look at him now.' I looked. The pig was standing at a point beside the cowl where a shower of sparks was escaping, in such a position that most of them impinged on his back. They bounced off him in all directions, covering him from nose to tail in a shimmering umbrella. On his face was an expression which was very like a smile. 'He loves that,' said my comrade. 'Like having his back scratched, I suppose. That's why they gave him the job really, not because he's much of a pig.' 'Oh?' I said. 'No, I have to set up for him, and put him right and so on. Mind you, he manages pretty well after that.'

Hanging on the wall between the two machines I saw a large notice covered in small type, headed 'Factories Act 1961 – Notes on the Employment of Pigs', beneath it in smaller type 'To be displayed in a prominent place wherever pigs are employed'. I walked over and looked at it. It was very long, but was divided into sections headed 'Safety', 'Health', 'Welfare', and 'Payment'. There was a paragraph on cleanliness, which stated that 'all accumulated dirt and refuse must be removed daily', and another which stipulated that every pig must have a minimum of 400 cu ft in which to work. There were paragraphs on temperature, ventilation, lighting, drainage of floors, 'Adequate Sanitary Accommodation' (which had to be separate for boars and sows) and facilities for sitting 'where sitting would not interfere with the work carried out'. Under 'Piecework Particulars' it said that every pig employed in piecework 'must have supplied to him such written particulars of the rates paid to him and the amounts of work done by him as to enable him to calculate the wage due to him'.

There was a good deal under 'Welfare'. Every pig must be properly and individually housed, together with family (if any), in a sound, weather-tight sty, in reasonable comfort, with adequate heating arrangements, space and privacy. He must be reasonably clothed, and be required to work not more than eight hours a day unless he wished to. He must receive sufficient food to enable him to carry out his duties to his employer without impairing his health in any way, 'and must be kept reasonably fat'. Under 'Payment' was the subheading 'Abstract of the Truck Act 1887', and this stated that 'every pig must be paid entirely in the proper swill of the realm'. At the very bottom was a paragraph headed 'Goads', stating that 'pigs shall not be poked or prodded or goaded in any way at all, or be frightened or otherwise coerced by any electrical device or bell or loudspeaker, either during working time or leisure time'.

I turned to the press operator. 'We live in an enlightened age,' I said. He said that he supposed we did, and that no doubt the wind of change was there to grasp, and after all weren't there things like instant coffee and hire purchase and worker shareholding for another thing. 'Do you hold shares in this company?' I asked. He stuck out his chest. 'I certainly do. I hold two penny shares and a ha'penny preference share. The pig bought five penny shares last week, which brings him up to eight. It gives you something to work for. I'm double time and treble time here most weeks now because I know I'm working for myself.' He came close to my ear. 'I wouldn't be surprised, if I work hard here for three or four years or so, that my tuppence ha'penny won't have doubled itself by that time. What do you think of that, eh? So much for your socialism!'

'You're working piecework here too,' I said. 'I've just been talking about piecework to a chappie further down.' 'Yes,' he said, 'That's why you'll have to excuse my carrying on work while I talk to you – it's just impossible to stop until a bell rings or something.' 'I'm sure it's a very great strain,' I said. 'Well, it is and it isn't,' he said. 'When you've a long run it's just like going to sleep really, except you're tired at the end of it. It's like being a puppet, you watch your hands and arms moving in front of you and doing the same things over and over and over again, and they don't seem part of you any more. Your legs too, and you get sort of disembodied, and float in mid-air. And after a bit your eyes go black – it's like being under an anaesthetic, I suppose.' 'Painless, then,' I said. 'Oh yes – except at certain times – when we change over jobs, for instance, and have to change the routine. We suffer agonies then, like a paralysed person learning to walk again, trying to take charge of your own body again. And all so that you can get paralysed again only in a different position. For a while there you find yourself doing crankcase covers like extruder nozzles, all one morning maybe. When you get an idea something is wrong you struggle and fight to get control and come to the surface to find out what's happened. That's when the agony comes. And then there are the worries, the worry that the time will sort of come over you from behind, like a surfrider who can't keep on top of the wave, or a hare trying to run downhill and falling over itself. You know, it's all cut down so fine, a sort of predetermination, so that with a few figures you know exactly when you'll have done ten, and then exactly when you'll have done twenty-five, and that when the bell rings you'll have your hands here and here and your feet so and so. It's all mapped out in front of you, every move and minute of it. It wouldn't be so bad if someone would come along and pat you on the back, or ask how many you've done, or take some interest. Come and have a chat, even. Sometimes I will something to go wrong with the bloody thing, just so that someone will come and look at it. You know,' he said, looking at me, 'you're the first person to come and stand here and talk to me for three months.'

'Really,' I said. He carried on working the machine

without faltering or pausing, while the ram rose and fell in perfect time. 'The last person was the foreman. He came to blow me up because I did 6,000 roller ends the wrong way round one morning. That wasn't very encouraging as the first human voice I'd heard since last Christmas. I can't talk to a pig. It's only enemies here. You're surrounded by enemies.' 'Enemies?' I said, surprised. 'Yes. He's the number one enemy round here,' he said, and pointed to the clock, a very large one which overlooked the whole shop. 'As you well know, he watches us all the time.' I said that I knew how he felt. 'Ah, but it's different with piecework. You don't do piecework, do you? You wouldn't know him as well as we do.' He looked up at the clock again. 'The old bastard. He's as tricky as an eel.' He shouted up at the clock, 'You wouldn't move at all if we didn't watch you, would you, you creeping bastard!' As if to answer him the clock clonked loudly and moved its minute hand an increment. He continued, quietly to me, 'And yet the more you watch the bugger the slower he goes. Clocks can hypnotise, you know – make you lose your sense of time.'

He came conspiratorially close, glanced up at the clock and said, 'Have you ever laid in bed just after the alarm goes off and tried to stare him out?' I shook my head, not understanding. 'No, you wouldn't have done it, you don't look that sort,' he put in quickly. 'But you think that if only you could concentrate hard enough and long enough and never take your eyes off the bastard for one second, you could stop him where he was – you know, like call his bluff, and make him go so slow between six-twenty and six-twenty-five that you could have a couple of hours lying in bed there, warm and snug.' But he shook his head and drew back from me as if the conspiratorial part of the conversation was now over. 'No, but you can't beat him at his own game,' he said with bitterness. Again addressing the clock: 'You're too tricky. You go like hell for some of us when we've got work to do, and drag all day for the rest of us – and then when we all come to look at you together you're at the same time for all of us – too crafty by half!' He turned back to me. 'It's frightening. You don't have your face rubbed in it like we do down here. Time. It's horrible. You people don't realise.'

I said I was sure it wasn't as bad as all that, but he insisted. 'Have you ever really experienced a minute, a whole minute? I mean, really have to live with it, to listen to it, every single second of it, nag, nag, nag, like a silly old woman.' He looked at me almost accusingly. 'Have you? Have you, eh?' I said I supposed I hadn't. He went on with great emotion, glancing at the clock quickly, 'You can hear your heart beating and your hair growing, and it's like walking on a long string bridge over a bottomless hole. You get to the middle, all suspended in thin air, and maybe you feel a bit dizzy and your heartbeat sounds a bit uncertain. You start to go from one heartbeat to the next like a tightrope walker, and maybe begin to lose your grip and fancy you might go spinning away into nothingness or eternity before you can get to the other side. It's dreadful.' His eyes bulged, 'And when you do make the other side you only find yourself going out on another tightrope before you've had a second to recover.' He put his hands over his ears and looked up at the clock. 'Move on, you bastard!' he shouted. He picked up a spanner and hurled it up at the clock, but it fell short and came down again with a jangle, hitting him on the shoulder. 'Move on!' he shouted. Mercifully the clock did so, with a loud clonk. He covered his face with his hands.

I didn't know what to do to help, and felt embarrassed, sure that everyone must be staring at us. I looked round, but everyone I could see was working, working like demons, jerking levers and running around the machines as if someone stood over them with a gun. I tried to change the subject of conversation. 'You must get good money here, all this regular piecework,' I said, enthusiastically. At this he burst out sobbing and laughing at the same time, so that I didn't know whether to smile or frown to appear in sympathy. 'No?' I said. If only I knew, he said. It was them, they fixed the rate for the job so efficiently, allowed for every variable so thoroughly, that there was nothing left for the operator to speed up on. There was an allowance made for setting up, another for emergency breakdowns, a deduction for the machine warming up, another for the operator warming up. 'They give me 12.6 minutes per day in the lavatory, and .62 minutes to scratch my left ear, which has a rash on it,' he said. 'There's an allowance for breathing and another for blowing my nose. If the rate looks good and might make me want to hurry, there's a special deduction, and there's an allowance for discouragement on Fridays. No variables left, nothing I can make money on – but I have to work like hell. Sometimes, when I've been running it neck-and-neck with the clock all day, I think bugger it all, I'm going off for a smoke. But then, all of a sudden in my mind's eye I see my wife and children all crashing about and breaking the furniture and smoking a hundred a day and peering in shop windows, and me sitting in the armchair with the kids climbing all over me and screaming for food, and the wife after a new slide-projector and what about an automatic tea-dispenser, and mother stamping about the house complaining of the cold and stoking up the fires fit to burn the house down, with the landlord knocking on the door for the second time this week and the bailiffs wanting the television – and, oh, my, I just forget all about the smoke and scuttle back here and go like hell to catch up with the few seconds I lost thinking about it.'

He sobbed quietly, then began again with anger, 'And all those adverts, too – they make me wild. I open the paper here and I know just what she'll be asking me for tonight, whose free offer for sixty guineas, what we just can't manage without any longer because everybody's got one. And me, well for me it's just as if I had to come here every day and make the bloody things, as if they were saying "Benjamin Jones, you must now go to work for nine months to make your wife the latest spin drier." That's what it's like really, isn't it?' I replied that I didn't really know enough about economics and so forth to say, but he said bugger the economics, it was as plain as the nose on your face. 'I'm sure it makes the money go round, or something,' I said. 'I don't care about the money,' he said, 'All I want is food and clothes and a bit of peace, and I could get that by coming here for one day a week. But with the wife and family and Radio Luxembourg my life isn't my own. Where's the glorious bloody freedom we fought for, then?' I said that I thought that we should all pull together and tighten our belts, hadn't the Prime Minister just said so? He laughed and said something very vulgar indeed about the Prime Minister, and asked me if I'd ever heard a Prime Minister who didn't say that every week. 'Trouble is the wife doesn't seem to listen,' he said bitterly.

I said I thought it was our duty to bring happiness to our families. 'Happiness?' he shouted. 'They don't know what happiness is. Their favourite pastime is rowing at me, and when I'm not there they row at each other. Just think, twenty million wives rowing with their husbands.' 'Surely it's not as bad as that,' I said. He asked me how I thought it was that you could get whole nations of men to go out and fight a war. 'To get a bit of peace,' he said. 'Like they say, War is Peace.' I asked him who said that. 'Chap called Tolstoy,' he replied. 'Probably a Communist,' I said. Then he started on about wars starting in the home and something about how every bad word was passed down from father to son for generation after generation until it all got too much, and then there would have to be war to clear it all up.

As he had been speaking to me he'd absentmindedly put

his hand underneath the punch to feel some part of the machine. I was reluctant to interrupt him, but had just decided that perhaps it was my duty to caution him, even at the expense of good manners, when the ram descended quickly and cut off his hand at the wrist as if it had been made of putty. He frowned and shook his head. 'That's what comes of talking too much.' Then smiling apologetically he said, 'I'm sorry, but you'll have to excuse me. I must go and report this. It is very important to report accidents to the accident steward immediately. He'll be very annoyed, I'm afraid – only last month he put up that poster' – he indicated with what would have been his finger a safety poster pinned on the wall nearby which bore the words 'Industrial Accidents cost money', superimposed on a picture of a worker in great distress with pound notes and silver coins pouring from a terrible gash in his stomach – 'and said a few words to all of us.' He came closer and confided, 'But he doesn't think of all the thousands of times that punch comes down every day without me letting it so much as trim my fingernails.' He stepped back and for a brief moment surveyed my reaction to his last statement, then, turning, he thrust his severed wrist into his pocket and stalked away.

Glancing at his machine I saw the hand lying underneath in the swarf box and shouted after him, 'Shouldn't you take this with you?' He stopped, turned, and asked me what I thought. 'I'm sure it's the proper thing to do,' I said, and added that I thought that they might even put it back if it hadn't got too dirty in the swarf box, since I'd read that such a thing had recently been done in Poland or somewhere. He came back. 'It would be some kind of proof, anyway,' he said. I pondered this statement, and was about to ask him what he meant when he suddenly reached down into the machine with his other arm. 'I've got it,' he said, but the punch came down and cut his arm off at the shoulder. 'Good heavens!' he exclaimed, and then, seeing my alarm, added

'– but we mustn't lose our heads.' I agreed, and said that perhaps after all it would be better if he left the hand where it was. He thought for a few seconds, then said, 'One, perhaps, but not two. Two is too many. My friend, would you be so good as to switch off this ridiculous machine and then go round behind it and lift out my limbs for me.' This I did willingly, and put his right hand into his left overall pocket and tucked his left arm under his right arm, while he told me that he was particularly annoyed at all this because he had another wife and several children on hire purchase and was already three weeks behind with the instalments. 'I may be forced to sell them,' he said, and again coming close to my ear, 'but they don't realise how often it doesn't happen.' He then thanked me and once again walked sadly away in the direction of the accident steward's office. I watched him go, and then decided to head the other way and try to find the stores.

I walked on for a long time through workshops where everyone was working piecework. No eyes here, nobody seemed to have time to so much as turn a head as I passed. I hurried on in the belief that eventually I should find someone I could speak to, someone who would have time enough to explain how to get to the General Parts Stores, and after covering a considerable distance I saw ahead of me a group of men chatting. As I came closer I saw that they were all standing around a small table, and when I finally reached them I noticed that on the table were playing cards, arranged in some kind of pattern. Thinking that I was interrupting a game I hesitated, but instantly the attention of everyone was turned on me. My embarrassment was increased by the action of the two men standing immediately to my right and left, who suddenly turned and took hold of both my arms in a grip as tight as two chain clamps. Then a man on the opposite side of the table who was taller than the rest shouted across to me, in quite a friendly voice, 'We can win, you know.' His use of the word 'we' gave me a clue – surely this was a works bridge or whist team. I was not particularly interested in card games, or any other sport, but a works team was rather different. 'You can win?' I asked. Everyone shouted, 'Yes, yes, win, we can win!' very loud, so that I didn't quite know what to say next. I said, 'How can you be so sure?' whereupon everyone fell into uneasy whispered consultation with everyone else. Only my guardians said nothing, and they did not relax their grip on me.

Then the whispering stopped and everyone turned back to face me, crowding in now, leaning over the table towards me until I could almost feel the bristly chins. Crabby grabby hands, some with one or two fingers missing, came sliding over the cards to touch my own hands. The men leaned across so close that I could smell them. They smelt of machine oil, and I could smell the smells of their homes, of homes like my own. I could smell the smells of cooking cabbage and burning milk, of fly-spray, stale tobacco smoke, mothballs and children's vomit, of hot soapy washing and unwashed dogs, of scorching linen and hot bakelite, of shoe polish, of cheap lavender brilliantine, of bad breath mixed with toothpaste, of deodorant and sweat, of dirty nappies and disinfectants and bleach and smoke and cats and soot and old people ill in bed.

The tall one spoke again, this time in a rasping whisper: 'A mascot.' 'A mascot?' I said, and a little man with an eye-shield over his left eye chirped, 'Yes, a horse, a golden horse with fifty legs and crystal hooves as big as dustbins, and his belly all horny and his sides all thorny and his back as big as Battersea Bridge.' 'Good heavens,' I said. 'Yes,' spoke up another man, 'and ears like spinnakers, and eyeballs like concrete mixers, and nostrils like spin driers and smelling like a tannery on a midsummer's day.' 'And his tail,' shouted another, 'is a flail of steel hawsers, and his jaws are the claws of mechanical grabs, and his hide is inch-thick boiler plate, and his mane is like a parade of the Coldstream Guards.' 'Yes,' called another, 'and horns on his head like Jodrell Bank.' 'My goodness gracious me,' I said. Another man shouted almost angrily, 'You could ride him round the earth in elliptical orbits blowing a golden trumpet,' and another, 'Or tidy up the stars a bit!'

Straight away they fell into discussion about whether they should actually show me this creature. With much frenzied nodding they decided yes, and the big man, with great flourish, produced a huge packet of breakfast cereal from under his waistcoat and started to try to open it, but it seemed to be very difficult. He struggled for some seconds until another big man who was sitting beside him snatched away the packet impatiently and tried to open it himself. He, however, had great thick fingers like blobs of plasticine, and he only succeeded in squashing the packet out of shape. Everyone shouted, 'Be careful, be careful, you great clumsy oaf,' and several people grabbed at the packet. A long thin man with only one arm managed to secure it, and tried to open it by tearing at it with his teeth. I saw that it was clearly marked at the top 'Open by pulling here', but it would not yield. Everyone grew dreadfully angry and started to shout. Half of them urged him to use more force while the other half cautioned him to use more care, while everyone near the man made grabs at the box. The operation became a tug-o'-war between three men; then suddenly the packet burst open and we were all showered with tiny pieces of flour paste in the forms of tanks and flowers and submarines. The three men dived at the torn packet and groped about inside it, until one leapt up grasping a cockroach between his thumb and forefinger. He held it up high and shouted out, 'Here he is, here he is, look at him, oh, isn't he splendid,' but someone else shouted angrily, 'It's dead, you clumsy fools, you've squashed it.'

And indeed it was dead, with its legs all twisted out of line and its head half off. Everyone roared with anger, but the man held the cockroach in front of his face and squinted at it, and said over and over again, 'It doesn't look dead to me, it doesn't look dead to me,' until everyone was so angry that they started to blame everyone else they could see and fighting broke out. Someone tried to tip over the table, and the cards were scattered. At this point the men who had been holding me let go to join in, so I took the opportunity of slipping away up the corridor.

It must have been sometime after this, when I had gone quite a long way and had had to admit to myself that I was completely lost, that I tripped and fell, although I don't remember doing so.

chapter three

First thing of all I'm always conscious of a wheel – or perhaps before that I'm conscious of spinning, in the abstract as it were, but then there is always this huge wheel all shimmering with lights and divided into segments of light, and a loud singing or humming noise. The wheel is not turning fast, but not slowly either, and it doesn't turn in one particular direction but both ways at once. After a time of spinning and shimmering and singing a kind of feeling of unease comes in. I can recollect all these things quite plainly, it's always the same. The wheel gets clearer, and there's more uneasiness, until there's suddenly fear, and a feeling of being stuck or paralysed and pinned in, like waking up to find you're inside a concrete block and you can't breathe or move or see or shout or anything. Yes, that's exactly what it's like. The wheel is still there and the humming noise gets louder, and then there's a moment of panic, of complete holy terror, that, wherever and whatever this situation is, it will go on for ever, for eternity, and I, a living breathing thing, will remain suspended in this black void, this halfworld, struggling to remember something but understanding only a singing, a wheel and my own paralysis for ever and ever. At that moment I usually open my eyes to find people suspended perpendicularly to me with their huge feet next to my ears and their faces turned towards me at the other end of them, so that I feel like saying, 'Whatever are you people all doing standing on the ceiling like that?' Then I remember who I am and where I am and everything is all right.

But this time when I opened my eyes there were no anxious people. This time I was coming round in Hell itself, or so it seemed. Before my eyes opened I smelt it quite distinctly, the stink of Hell: smoke and sulphur and that peculiarly unpleasant smell of burning hair or flesh. Then my ears heard the sound of Hell, as loud and relentless as the noises of my own department of the factory, but quite different in character. There was a continuous roar so deep that the ground shook like cardboard under my body, and another roar like steam escaping from terrible pressure. Somewhere an unearthly hammer was pounding the ground quickly and ceaselessly. Great grindings and crashings, like gigantic rocks colliding, and the howl of a circular saw as big as the moon. Then I felt the heat striking my skin, but it was not painfully hot, only uncomfortably so.

I became fully conscious and opened my eyes to see all the fire of Hell as if I had never seen fire before. I saw walls built of bricks of it, I saw three towers of it, with square windows all the way up through which protruded giant ostrich feathers of even brighter flame, so that the fire itself seemed to be on fire. There were rivers and waterfalls of blinding fire and flower-pots from which grew swaying trees of it. Creatures moved about in twos and threes, glowing red and big as bulls, licking out with sudden bright tongues, while others sulked darkly in corners. All around me regiments of little rabbity creatures with dancing ears stuck their shining heads out of the ground, which was alive with skipping, sparkling insects. Tiny jewelled firebirds dropped out of dreadful rolling clouds above me which were sometimes blackest black and sometimes incandescent red.

Suddenly out of one such cloud came a manlike creature of the same changing red and black. Surely the Devil. He was vast and round in the body, with a tall chimney-like head and great club feet, and he bore a cauldron of fire alive with fiery grasshoppers and flaming like a meteor. Presently he stopped and tipped the cauldron slowly and fire ran from it like treacle into a huge box, which instantly burst at all its seams with blue and yellow flames. I remember that suddenly I felt as if I had known all along that some such fate as this would overtake the earth, and I wanted to get up and slap someone on the back and say, 'I told you so' – but in fact I had never told anybody so, and felt rather peculiar about it, as if in some way this had all been brought about by me in some final and vindicating revenge on the world for I wasn't quite sure what. Had my wife, then, been so selfish, my children so irksome, my mother-in-law so unreasonable, my marriage so hollow, and had the life to which all these and my employers had condemned me for so long been so futile, that it took all this to atone for it? I might embrace the answer Yes! and leap up and run round with the Devil in a frenzy of revenge, pouring buckets of fire into boxes of my relations, of criminals and young men who hit old ladies over the head, and layabouts, communists and Germans, of hairy-chested men and fierce dogs, and of sexy young girls who laughed at you behind your back, and interfering children who climbed over fences, and people who always pushed in front. The Devil had finished pouring and raised his arms as if to conduct the whole hellish orchestra to its final crescendo. I could not bear it. I jumped up, and realised that I was in the foundry.

Wife and family all dropped back into their proper places, and I felt very much relieved. Of course all things have a rational explanation, and even the Devil turned into a man, who took off his goggles and came over to me laughing. 'So you're up,' he shouted above the din. 'Ran in and fell over a cope. Have a fag, here.' He produced a lighted cigarette from nowhere and stuck it between my lips, then guided me over to a small table around which were five battered old chairs. 'Sit down,' he ordered. I did so, and he sat himself, a good distance from the table to allow room for his paunch, which was enormous. Three other men approached the table from different directions. It was quite dark over here further from the furnaces, and each man was heralded by the glow of his cigarette, homing in on the table like a glowworm. They all sat, in that automatic casual way of men who sit on the same chair in the same place at the same time of day every day for years and years, and unfolded their newspapers, blowing out fast clouds of smoke as they relaxed. They took no notice of me, but all read the same page of identical newspapers, and turned the pages simultaneously.

The youngest was very young, new to the place obviously. Thin and scrawny with ears two sizes too big for him and spots. No chin, hair combed back impeccably. He looked as if he spoke with a squeaky voice and a stupid grin. They always did, and blushing and stammering so that you couldn't resist kicking them about. Well, not exactly kicking, much more humorous than that. I didn't go in for it much myself, but some of the men made quite a thing of it, a kind of tradition. I often wondered how it was that these boys could ever become real factory workers, they always seemed so weedy – but they'd always turn into some kind of man before very long, and swear as hard as the next.

I looked at the next man along, opposite me, and tried to imagine what he was like. He was obviously a clown type. Always good to work with, one of those men who seem to have an inexhaustible catalogue of jokes stored away in their heads – some of them not exactly in the best of taste but always very entertaining. And always ready to sympathise too, when someone else was being awkward. This man was fat and with all his features chewed up and pushed into the middle of his face like currants – two little curranty eyes so close together that you couldn't have got a penny between, and a sultana for a nose. The third man was long and thin and private-looking, with one eye in the centre of his head, and he was covered in dirt, with dirt in his sprouty hair. The man who had given me a cigarette was as big as all the other three put together, he was an elephant. His main mass was concentrated in his paunch, and he leaned back in his chair uncomfortably as women do in the later stages of pregnancy. His belly moulded his trousers and the lie of his belt so that the latter was forced to swoop down to his crutch at the front, and his flies, long despaired of ever meeting, flapped outwards like wings. His head was tall and cylindrical like a chimney-pot, which swivelled about as he read the paper. All of them exhaled cigarette smoke in great clouds.

'Aries,' announced the fat curranty man without looking up. ' 'Arry who?' said the apprentice, and grinned. 'If you say that once more I'll kick your arse for you,' said the curranty-man, whose name was Fred. 'Only trying to be funny,' said the apprentice. 'Joe,' went on Fred, 'Your initiative will pay off.' Joe laughed a deep gurgling laugh which shook his great stomach and set his flies flapping, a laugh without any humour, a laugh which was a jeer; but Fred persisted, 'It's pools coming up, Joe. But you could pay dearly for a thoughtless act or careless word,' he added, looking at the paper again. 'K'cher!' hiccoughed Joe, and threw down the remains of his cigarette and ground it into the floor with his foot. 'Now 'Arry's,' said Fred, and glowered at the apprentice, who giggled. He turned to the one-eyed man. 'Affairs of the heart will –' Joe cut him off. 'Wrap up with your silly old woman's bloody fairy tales,' he roared. 'It's all made up by some bloody queer who earns more in a week than you do in a month, you know that as well as I do.'

He threw down his own copy of the paper and stamped on it. 'Fucking nonsense and bloody fairy tales,' he shouted, while the other three looked nervous and rustled their own papers as if they weren't sure if they shouldn't do the same. 'Look at this!' Joe grabbed the paper out of the hands of the one-eyed man and slammed it down on the table. 'Look at it.

Look at those women. Look at that one.' He crashed his hand down on a photograph of a near naked girl lying on a deserted beach in sunshine. 'And that,' he shouted, indicating another woman at the wheel of a sports-car. The others looked and then at him with puzzlement. 'And the money, look at the money.' He grabbed the paper up and started to scan through it. 'Look – bank raid, twenty thousand pounds.' The others looked. 'Twenty thousand pounds!' he roared at them, as if they hadn't understood. 'And look at this – "Smarty Wiseman sues Benny Catchpenny for half a million!" And look, all the magistrates in London have just got a rise of more than we earn!' he bellowed. 'And look at those bastards living it up!'

'Well,' said Fred, after Joe had been glowering at them for some seconds. Joe put out his hands like an exasperated deaf mute. 'Harry' – Harry looked at him with his eye – 'how much do you earn?' 'About ten bob less than you,' said Harry glumly. His mouth only opened on the left side, which gave him a dishonest look when he spoke, as if he were trying to talk to the people on his left without those on his right hearing. Joe went on, 'And how much do you think you might possibly earn if you were lucky?' 'Well, if you were to drop dead they might make me foreman and then I'd have as much as you.' 'If you were lucky,' returned Joe. 'If I was lucky.' 'Well, there's an advert here,' said Joe, mauling the paper, 'for an assistant managing director starting at fifteen hundred a year!' 'What's that a week?" squeeked the apprentice, lighting another cigarette. 'Thirty quid!' hissed Joe. 'Christ,' said the apprentice, and whistled out a gust of smoke. 'There's always the pools,' said Fred. 'Kah!' sneered Joe. 'The pools – they just dangle a bloody great sum of money in front of you and you go on paying out your five bob 'til kingdom come, to keep some other lazy bugger fat!'

Harry said quickly, 'I never met anyone anywhere who ever won anything. I don't think anyone ever wins anything.'

Joe exploded then, 'But they do, Harry,' he shouted. 'This bloody paper's full of it. Money, money, money.' As he said these words he crushed the paper up into a ball and, holding it in his fists, smashed it on to the table three times and then threw it down. 'A bloody curse,' he roared, 'on everyone with more money than me!' They all looked glum, then Joe snatched up Fred's paper. 'Look,' he said, 'all this bloody fucking and fornication. Who's married who for the fifth time, who Smarty Wiseman is going about with now, sex parties on yachts, cabinet minister's mistresses. How do they get away with all this fucking and no kids?' He brought both his fists down on the table with a crash. 'I've got half-a-dozen kids to cope with from living with one woman, let alone six or seven.' 'Don't you know?' sniggered the apprentice. 'Oh yes,' jeered Joe across the table. 'I know about that all right. We've spent a small fortune on those things in twenty years, but we've still got a houseful of brats. I know why the bloody Indians and wogs don't use 'em – they can't afford 'em.' 'It's those envious bastards making holes in them,' said Harry glumly. 'Well what is it, then?' said Fred. 'It's the money!' shouted Joe. 'You don't have kids if you've got plenty of money, and what you do have you pay someone else to look after.'

Joe had been shouting all this time as if everyone had been disagreeing with him, although no one had. Men in our shop sometimes did that, for no good reason at all. I've seen men talk to each other and then rant and rave and end up fighting like tigers, and yet every word they said was in agreement with every other, no difference of views at all. The words don't matter really, the opinions themselves aren't important. Or you can be grumbling about the weather, which you can't blame anyone for. I've been involved in arguments like that myself; sometimes they're difficult to get out of when the air is bad, so to speak, everyone on edge. Someone accuses you of something or challenges you in front of the others, and you don't know if he's just having a joke or being really nasty. You daren't show that you think he's serious, because if he's not you'll look a fool in front of the others, but you have to defend yourself in case he is, so you answer him back in a way which could be interpreted as serious or not serious, whichever suits the situation. But then he probably finds himself in the same position as you were, and doesn't know whether to take you seriously and apologise, in which case he might look rattled in front of the others, or call your bluff, or defend himself or what – so he says something even more outrageous, calculated to be taken either as a genuine insult or as an even more extravagant piece of buffoonery, whichever suits.

And so it goes on, each one going a little bit further each time until suddenly it gets out of hand and the fists are flying. I've seen good friends start fighting like that. Then a crowd might collect, and everyone would say they should settle it with a fair fight; everyone likes to see a good fight, fair or not, when they're feeling like that, it always helps. That's why all factory workers go home at night and get glued to their sets to see a good wrestling match or boxing. I believe that when world championships are televised there isn't a factory worker in the country with a television set who doesn't sit up until two o'clock if necessary to see them, and the next day at work there's only one topic of conversation. So they try to arrange a proper fight when the chance presents itself, but then that brings it down to a more cold-blooded level and the would-be fighters often make excuses or divert attention, by starting an argument over whether it should be a boxing match or a judo or a wrestling match. Very soon everyone is quarrelling with everybody else about whether the world's champion boxer would beat the world's champion wrestler or not if they were put together, and presently everyone would get angry enough to put everyone in the world, every single man and boy scrapping and fighting together until they've all knocked each other's brains out except one, who'd be king of the world and all the women in it.

Joe folded Fred's paper, tore it into little pieces and threw it on to the floor, then lit another cigarette. Harry and Fred smoked away, newspaperless, like naked. Only the apprentice still read on, turning the pages frequently and skipping backwards and forwards through the thing like a child pretending to read. Suddenly he read out, 'Are you a cruncher or a sucker?' in a loud Radio Luxembourg voice. The other two watched Joe discreetly, but there was no response. At length Harry said, 'Sweets are for kids, stupid.' 'Not here,' chirped back the apprentice. 'Here it says that sweets are for lively young-minded up-to-the-minute young people like you darling. You darling is in big letters.' 'Gah!' exploded Joe, and everyone, including myself, flinched as he lunged across the table to snatch the apprentice's paper. 'Dreams!' he roared, and raised the paper above his head. 'Dreams for the bloody workers!' and he beat the paper on the table again and again as if he were beating the life out of a dog, until nothing was left of it but the piece he gripped in his hand.

He walloped his two fists on the table and heaved himself out of the chair so that he leaned forward, thrusting his face into ours. 'Anywhere you go,' he said quietly, 'in this factory, you'll find men reading this paper. This paper, not any other. There's ten to choose from,' he said, and catching something in Fred's eye, 'yes, I know I read it too; I've read it for thirty years. I've sat at this table,' he hissed, and raised his fists up in front of his face, 'at this time every day for thirty years' – all eyes were raised to his fists – 'and read that bloody paper.' He put his fists slowly back on to the table again, and the others relaxed. His knuckles crunched as he leaned his weight on them. 'Read the news,' he went on quietly, glaring at each of us in turn, 'the news of a world where charladies win fortunes, where ships sink with all hands, or men make daring rescues, or fight and die for their country.' His voice rose a little. 'Photographs of the world's best fucks, stories of men like us who make fortunes. Stuff about cars; stuff about sport' – all eyes were on his fists, but they did not leave the table – 'stuff about football pools; stuff about criminals; stuff about people with money enjoying themselves.' There was a second of silence, during which no one dared to move. Joe began again, and his fists began to rise. The eyes followed them. 'So here we are,' he shouted, 'all the bloody millions of us whose lives are just home and work, home and work every day for all of our decent bloody lives' – the fists were up – 'kept happy' – everyone cringed, waiting for the fists – 'by the vicarious' – he was bawling – 'Daily, Bloody, Dream!' and as quick as a flash he grabbed the table and tipped it over, throwing everyone into confusion, then turned and strode away towards the furnaces.

As we picked ourselves up I thought that since I was feeling much better now I should say goodbye to everyone and carry on with my search for the stores. We sat down again and I explained that I must be going, but Fred said, 'Aw, relax' and offered me another cigarette, and said that I should wait for Joe to come back before leaving. I looked over towards the furnaces. There was Joe, silhouetted against the fires, distinguishable by his enormous bulk and peculiar shape from hordes of smaller men, who looked like negroes, though it was difficult to tell, and swarmed about in all directions. The thoughts of Hell returned: he might have been the Devil surrounded by a legion of devils, scuttling around on devilish business at the centre of Hell. He waved his arms about and the devils ran like sheep turned this way and that by the dog. Some held long iron rods with hooks at their ends, some pushed trucks and skips along, some pulled big levers and some turned great wheels. Then I saw Joe, giant among pygmies, pick up a great hooked pole like a rugby post and reach up with it to some point high above them. There was a roll of thunder and instantly a long strip of fire appeared across their ankles and grew into a long rectangle. A door was lifting like a vast mouth opening, wider and wider until it was as high as it was broad, as high as Joe's pole. The men ran about silhouetted at the bottom of it like flies at the bottom of a window pane, and in the centre stood Joe, gesturing with his arms. Enormous tongues of flame curled out to him, thunder shook the ground and great blobs of fire like sun jumped out and exploded in showers of sparks around their legs. As I watched I saw several of the negroes take up poles and, as Joe pointed, charge like raving soldiers into the inferno itself, to be swallowed up, or so it looked to me. At another peel of thunder Joe turned to those on the other side of him and pointed an arm at them, and they too stormed into the fire, dragging and pushing their trucks or charging with poles. As they disappeared huge clouds of glowing gases gushed out and up. Now Joe reached in the air with both his arms, and others ran into the fire carrying giant spoons or ladles. After that there were practically no more men left, and Joe strode over to the side of the cavern and pulled on a great wheel.

'You shouldn't be afraid of Joe,' said Fred to me. I said that I thought he was rather a fine fellow of a man. 'Oh, it's just his way of talking,' said Fred, 'you shouldn't take him too seriously, he's got a heart of gold. He's just letting off steam. Does a man good to watch him sometimes.' Joe was heaving down on the wheel and presently I saw that the whole rectangle was tipping, turning slowly on its corner. Its contents seemed to swirl and splash about, and why Joe had not been roasted alive or set on fire by the flames and the sparks I could not imagine. 'You sit tight when he comes back and we'll give you a full performance,' said Fred.

Suddenly a line of blinding fire streaked out from the mouth of the furnace like an arrow, like a neon tube switched on. At its far end it curled over and hung there flaming and spitting sparks. The furnace was pouring. 'Performance?' I queried. 'You'll see,' said Fred. 'His dream is what he would do to the manager if he had the chance.' Even Harry chuckled. The line thickened and was painful to look at. I could feel the heat of it from where I was sitting. I could see the outline of the tremendous cauldron which was being filled, and the glow which came from its mouth, lighting up clouds of smoke passing high above us all. The others watched, and the light turned their faces to devilish masks of polished silver and gold, with smoke streaming out of their nostrils and mouths. Why was I sitting here? I had work to do. 'It'll do you good to watch it,' promised Fred.

Presently the furnace tipped back, the stream vanished, the door closed again to a narrow strip, which disappeared; only the fiery light of the cauldron remained, which was now full. Joe came striding back to the table with a cigarette glowing in his mouth, and sat down again. He pulled a newspaper from his pocket and unfolded it, and to my astonishment I saw that the other three also had newspapers which they were unfolding. They all turned the pages simultaneously as before, and I thought that we had somehow slipped back in time, until Fred said, 'Yes, I suppose none of it's real really, is it?' No one looked up. He read out, '"Clacton landladies strip in fight over sewage."' He blew smoke out of his nostrils. 'That's not really about our world, is it?' Harry asked him if he thought it was about Mars. 'No,' said Fred, 'its like Joe said, it's all made up.' 'It's the news,' argued Harry, and read out as if to prove his point, '"Shot Briton Grilled."' 'Well?' said Fred. Harry read on, '"Communists grilled RAF Corporal Douglas Johns in Potsdam yesterday."' Fred asked him if he believed it. 'Well, of course I do,' said Harry vehemently. 'This is a newspaper, it reports the bloody news.'

Fred scanned his paper. '"Row in Parliament,"' he read

out. 'There you are, then, that's not real.' 'Well, of course it is,' said Harry. 'Have you ever seen the Prime Minister?' Harry said no, he'd never actually seen him, but he'd seen his photograph in the papers. 'Well, there you are then,' said Fred triumphantly. 'Like all these earthquakes and big fires you read about,' he went on, warming up. 'Always a big fire, somewhere, on the telly – see the smoke and the firemen and the people jumping and so on. Then you straight away go over to an advert for salad cream or something. I mean it's not real, is it?' Harry stubbed out his cigarette and lit up another. Fred went on, 'You come to work and everything's just the same, nothing's changed. Everybody's there, everyone says good morning, just as they always do. Nothing feels any different. We all come to this table at half-past ten, and smoke and read our papers, Just like we always do.' No one looked up; they might not have been listening. Fred shouted, 'Nothing's different!'

There was a pause while the other three looked up slowly, and Fred suddenly looked embarrassed, as if he regretted shouting. Joe spoke, quietly and with a little menace. 'What do you mean, Fred, different?' Fred tapped his cigarette nervously. 'Well – well, you'd think you might feel different, creep around watching for something to happen...' he trailed off. 'Something to happen?' said Joe, as if Fred had said something which ought not to have been said. Fred made an awkward gesture. 'Those great big factory fires that burn whole factories down in half-an-hour, and people can't get out – then, as if dismissing himself, 'but it's like you say, Joe, it's not real, it couldn't happen here.' He puffed his cigarette and buried his curranty nose in his paper as if there was no more to be said.

But Joe would not let him get away. 'It could, you know,' he said quietly. The apprentice and Harry looked nervous, as if a thunderbolt was about to fall. Fred laughed unconvincingly. 'Nah, nah, it couldn't, it's like you say, Joe.'

There was a pause. 'How could it, Joe?' Fred waved his arm. 'Firebricks, look, and steel girders, and concrete. It couldn't burn down, there's nothing to burn.' 'It could, Fred,' said Joe. 'The girders would creak like wood, and the concrete crack like china, the bricks would bend like rubber and the iron would run like syrup.' Harry and the apprentice fidgeted and tried to hide in their newspapers. 'Nah, Joe,' whined Fred, 'same as houses. I had a look at my house. I looked at it, it couldn't burn down, it's nonsense to say that it could burn. It's bricks, Joe. Bricks don't burn.' 'Burn to the ground before you could get down the stairs, Fred,' said Joe, gently. 'Nah, Joe – not really.' 'And all the other houses in the street,' said Joe, snapping his fingers in the air, 'just like that!' 'It couldn't happen,' protested Fred, almost in tears. Joe went on, 'Every house from here to Blackpool smoking bloody rubble in the twick of an arse.' 'No!' shouted out Fred, and banged the table. He looked at Harry and the boy for support, but they were reading with their heads low. He was spluttering now, 'But not – not really – I mean solid – it's solid when I'm in my house, it's a lotta bloody nonsense – I mean look at all those houses and streets, Joe – and bridges, and shops – they're made up of bricks and concrete – do you mean to say you can look at all our town and believe that it could just catch fire and – and – well, disappear?' Joe nodded. 'It couldn't, Joe!' Fred shouted out, so that even the other two looked up.

There was silence, while Fred looked about as if he thought that the evidence floated in the air somewhere near him. 'You know, Fred,' said Joe, as if Fred was a child, 'the trouble with you is you've got no sense of humour –' But Fred was excited. He thumped Harry on the shoulder and shouted in his ear, 'Could they, Harry – you don't believe it, do you?' Harry said nothing. 'When you're at home in bed, warm in the dark with the missus, nothing can touch you!' He turned to Joe and screamed out, 'Can it, Joe? People don't burn, flesh and blood don't burn!' 'Don't you shout at me!' roared Joe.

There was a pause, then Joe went on – 'No bloody sense of humour, Fred. You've got to be able to laugh at these things.' 'Nothing, not really, you don't believe it, Joe,' moaned Fred, while Joe went on quietly, ''Laugh it off, don't let it get you down.' Fred moaned on, '– not come into yer house, Joe –' 'Shake up your tonsils, Fred' 'Say it's not real, Joe –' 'Tell us a joke, Fred,' demanded Joe. 'Do you know what I read, I read – I read –' 'A funny joke!' roared Joe, and jumped up and thrust his hand across the table, gripping Fred by his overall just under the throat. 'Tell!' he barked. Fred spluttered on, shaking his head about and pleading, while Joe shook him like a rag doll until his teeth chattered. 'Go on,' Joe roared, 'the one about the chap who couldn't get a stand –' but Fred was going on about skin peeling off or something. 'So he went to the doctor,' prompted Joe. 'Go on.' 'Half the doctors were dead!' Fred cried out, whereupon Joe grabbed him with both hands and dragged him up out of his seat. 'Tell us a bloody joke or I'll smash your bloody skull!' he roared, with his face right up to Fred's.

At this point a little black man came across and called Joe away to the furnaces, leaving Fred in a heap on the table. The other two helped him off and dusted him down – though I don't know why – and he seemed quite normal again immediately. I made up my mind to leave them then, having seen enough unpleasantness; but when I tried to go they begged me to stay and hear Joe talk about the manager, which I did not want to do in the slightest after what had just happened. But Fred said that it would do me a power of good, and they sat me down and made me smoke another cigarette. Joe was striding across the shop with the cauldron following behind him like a flying carthorse, and presently he arrived at the next box and positioned the huge crucible over it. Then he tipped it slowly with the aid of a wheel, and out came the metal in a shining stream, setting the flames leaping and the sparks dancing on the floor and in the air around him. When the cauldron was empty he pushed it back to the furnace, and presently rejoined us.

In order, I fancied, to prevent Joe from resuming where he had just left off, Fred put the question to him almost before he had sat down, whereupon he did not sit down but seized the table in both hands, lifted it above his head and slammed it down behind Harry. Then he picked up his chair and placed it on the other side of the table. What happened then is beyond relating, although it started reasonably enough. Fred persuaded me that it would be a good idea if I sat in the chair to represent the manager, which I did; and then Joe, pretending I was the manager, demonstrated what he would do if he ever had the chance to speak to him face to face. He said some very thought-provoking and challenging things, while the others stood and listened and passed remarks of criticism or encouragement. I thought that it would add to the effect if I acted up the part, so after a while I told Joe, quite sharply, to address me as Sir. This took him quite by surprise, and the other three laughed heartily; so when Joe began to swear a little, I said, as convincingly as I could, that I would not tolerate such language in my office; whereupon the others jeered and cheered, and I found that I was quite enjoying myself, and told them all, after a particularly blistering onslaught by Joe, that they would all get their cards if they weren't careful. The apprentice and Fred then started to get excited, and I must have got rather carried away myself, because in the end I was forced to run for my life with all four of them chasing me, and the language was dreadful, though I, who have been familiar with the worst of factory language for sixteen years, say it.

chapter four

I sized up the operator of a nearby cylindrical grinder, but he looked too surly and I walked on. The machine beyond, a vertical lathe, didn't seem to be working, and the next operator was so busy at his mill that I didn't like to disturb him. Then came a horizontal borer, and the operator would certainly have time to speak to me, I thought. But when I drew level with him he was surrounded by a group of men, some of whom were in white coats and some of whom held stop-watches, and they were all craning their necks over his shoulders like vultures so I couldn't disturb him. On the machine opposite two men were struggling with a heavy jig, but further up, on a flypress, was a very pleasant-looking man, and I spoke to him. He smiled and seemed very polite, but he was a Pakistani or a Chinese, and didn't speak a word of English. The next man along was also very polite, but he had no idea where the General Parts Stores was, and the man opposite him, who was operating a great capstan lathe all running and splashing with coolant water, wasn't polite at all, and swore at me and said that he hadn't time to talk to people who had nothing better to do than walk about the factory looking for places they couldn't find and poking their noses where they weren't supposed to be and disturbing people who hadn't the time to talk to them. 'No wonder I have to work so bloody hard,' he finished up, 'if I have to carry people like you,' and he slammed the lathe into gear as if he wanted to strip the teeth off every sprocket in the box.

After that I resolved to disturb no one who was busy, but now it seemed that everybody was. After passing many men very hard at work I noticed that nobody was actually working their machines; everyone was occupied at tasks which would, I thought, normally have been done by the labourers in the section. One man was clearing up a heap of shavings and empty condensed-milk tins, another had left his machine to distribute protective leather gloves to everyone nearby. Another was clearing away pools of dirty oil from around the machines with the aid of sawdust and a shovel, and a group of men were engaged in jamming various old rejected components and disused jigs into cupboards, which were too small to take them, so that they couldn't get the doors closed and had to repeatedly repack the cupboards, throwing glances over their shoulders as they did so. Another man was trying to persuade a number of young boys to climb into a cupboard, while nearby a man was covering a big hole in the floor with broomsticks and newspapers. But most of the men were at their machines doing only one thing – fitting the guards. Ancient guards of every shape and size were being dragged out from under cupboards and dusted down and oiled, and then with great haste and brandishing of spanners being fitted over their respective cutters or pulleys, or gears. Here and there, where a nut or a bolt was missing, the fixture was made good with lengths of hairy string, and one guard had been entirely improvised from corrugated cardboard. Everyone was busy to the point of frenzy, and almost everybody had developed a habit of intermittently looking quickly over his shoulder as he worked.

I knew very well what all this meant. Further up the gangway in front of me a little party was moving along in this direction. It was comprised of the local factory inspector, a little old stooped man who wore dark glasses and carried a white stick, and a number of members of the factory staff, who helped the little man along by holding his arms on either side and gently pushing him from behind. As they came closer I saw that the old man was fumbling about with one hand trying to find the earpiece of his hearing aid, which dangled about on the end of a white cord. With his other hand he was clutching both his white stick and a bundle of papers, some of which slipped out from time to time and fluttered away. His escort, all dressed in charcoal or Drunge green suits and shining white collars, chattered to him about this and that, cars, the bank rate, living in the country versus living in the town, the price of a new suit, and so on, but all together so that the old man couldn't possibly have heard even if his earpiece had been in. Presently he did find it, and when it was securely in place he said something in a squeaky breathless voice about having to stop and make some notes.

They stopped, and he fumbled about with his bundle of papers, finally giving them to one of the party. Then he dug around in his overcoat pocket and found a little stub of a pencil which he also gave to the man, who had a breast pocket crammed with writing instruments. 'Be so good,' croaked the old man, 'as to mark them off where I tell you to.' 'Certainly,' said the clerk or whatever he was. The old man tip-tapped about impatiently with his stick. 'What have you got here, then?' he said, staring down the gangway with his black glasses. Everyone at the machines stood lounging about, but they were careful to make no sounds. 'Just a few old benches and so forth,' said one of the clerks. 'Old?' chirped up the old man. The clerk hastily said that they weren't very old, quite new in fact, and this seemed to satisfy the old man, who fumbled about for a few seconds and then asked if anyone had seen where he had put his papers. They told him, and he said, 'Oh yes – well, mark that off for me, will you?' The clerk said, Yes, he would and then the old man said, 'Have you done it yet?' and the clerk said that he had, whereupon the old man said that he hadn't heard the pencil squeak. 'That's because your hearing aid has fallen out,' said another of the group. The old man asked him to repeat that, which he did, and then the whole party moved off chuckling and joking, the old man croaking, 'Ha ha! You won't catch me out so easily, you young scallywags!' and the others exclaiming, 'My goodness gracious me, no, sir!' and pushing him along.

Now at least I can ask someone the way I thought, but immediately the men began working even more busily, dismantling the guards and emptying the cupboards, and not a labourer to be seen anywhere. I trudged on.

When at last I was forced by desperation to speak to a man who was working, he was not in the least annoyed; in fact when he saw me open my mouth to speak he spoke first. 'It's a long day, isn't it?' he said. 'Yes,' I replied. There are many such statements in factory conversation, to which the answer is always yes, because they are not so much statements of opinion or fact as they are expressions of a kind of unity. It might be technically correct to reply, 'Today is exactly the same length as yesterday,' or 'You cannot reasonably say that the gauge is wrong,' or 'The manager works very hard,' or 'But it would be impossible to have intercourse in the office in the lunch break' – but it would definitely not be polite. The proper answer in all cases is, 'Yes, you are right,' for such is the convention, and no purpose is served by going against it. I remember, years ago, a very young man who suddenly took it into his head to refuse to say 'Good morning' to everyone in the customary way. He said that it was meaningless because everybody knew that it wasn't a good morning at all because they were all at work, and that it was hypocrisy, too, to wish people a good morning when you knew you'd be sneering and carping at them behind their backs before the teabreak had started. Of course he was technically right – but he nearly had a nervous breakdown, and finished up on his knees begging people to say good morning to him. He had to leave, and I never did hear what became of him.

This man was operating a shaper. A shaper is perhaps the only other machine for which it is possible to feel some kind of affection. They are immensely strong machines, but also dignified, and I have heard them likened to old carthorses. You can pat their backs in the same sort of way. I suppose you could ride on them if you wanted to, though I have never seen anybody but an apprentice try, and that was at Christmas when he was drunk, and of course he fell off and spoilt his Christmas. A shaper consists of a great horizontal reciprocating ram which moves comparatively slowly but with great force across a bed to which the component is clamped. A single small cutting tool is mounted on the nose of the ram, and the bed may be moved, by means of handles connected to screws, in any direction. Usually the machine is set working with the ratchet selfact engaged, so that each time the ram withdraws the component is moved forward a suitable increment, while the operator sits on a stool and smokes. Each time the ram moves forward it strips up a long curling shaving which crackles and sings as it grows, and often changes colour quite delightfully. At the end of the stroke the shaving is pushed over the end of the bed to land in exactly the same place as its predecessor, while the ram draws back for the next stroke and the ratchet moves the table across another fraction. Unfortunately such machines are growing rarer now that mills are being made which are big enough and powerful enough to straddle even the largest castings with a single cutter, thereby saving time. In the interests of progress we must see both the carthorse and the shaper disappear from the land.

But this man didn't seem to share my affection for the machine. He was younger than I was, although everything seemed to be working perfectly well he kept fidgeting about with the controls, and checking the depth of cut and so on. When I spoke about the machine he asked me if I'd ever operated one. I said that I hadn't really, although years ago, when I first came to work in the factory, an old man who chewed tobacco let me work his shaper after he'd told me all about it, and I used to oil it for him on Friday nights because he couldn't get at all the pots. 'Well, you work one for a bit before you make up your mind,' he said. 'Is it boring?' I asked. 'It gets on my nerves,' he said, 'it makes my fingernails itch.' 'Good gracious,' I said, and noticed that his nails were all bitten short and bleeding. 'Sometimes,' he went on, 'when I've been watching the ram go backwards and forwards, backwards and forwards for an hour or so, and thinking how strong it must be to peel off that shaving as easily as that, and how cleverly designed the whole machine is, and what a marvellous thing electricity must be to come along that little wire like that without so much as a twitch and then make this bloody great machine work; sometimes, when I've been thinking about all these things for a long while, I suddenly get afraid that the component is going to jump out with the force of the cut, and the tool break and bend the ram and jam up the gears and burn out the motor. It comes over me all in a wave, and I go hot and cold all over and hold on to my chair, or keep grabbing at the stopping handle. Sometimes I even stop the machine in the middle of the cut, which is worse. It waits there with its nose down and the shaving half made, chugging away and waiting for me to start it again. And starting it in the middle of a cut really can be difficult.'

He paused to make a few adjustments to the ratchet feed, which looked perfectly all right to me. Then he went on, 'If the component did jump off the chances are that nothing very serious would happen, it would probably just get pushed over the end of the bed, and I'd get a break putting it back. But there'd be a bang and everyone would look – everyone always does when there's a bang – and I'd go all red and shaky and wouldn't know which lever to pull first, and

I'd try to stop the machine although it would already have stopped itself, and then I'd start cleaning it down – it's funny, you find yourself cleaning your machine down when anything upsetting happens.' I said that I did seem to recollect that being so myself. 'And then,' he went on, 'when I was putting things back the labourer would come across and lean on his broom like those people who crowd round when there's a road accident to see the blood, and ten to one I wouldn't understand what he'd say, because he's a Pole and I never do, and he'd repeat it over and over again until I'd get all embarrassed and desperate and I'd repeat the sounds exactly to try to help him and he'd think I was mimicking him and get upset.' 'Dear me,' I said. 'It's all silly, I know that,' he replied, 'but nerves are nerves.'

'What's the cause of it all?' I said. 'Why, the boredom, of course,' he replied. 'I get so bored here I don't know where to look. I've seen it all, every face, every machine, every brick in the bloody wall, every mark on the floor. I just don't know what to do with my eyes. I read the newspaper six times before ten, and do the crossword. I know every possible combination of noughts and crosses, I've made little rockets out of matches and silver paper, I've played five-stones and cats-cradles and every game under the sun, I've caught flies and pulled their wings off, I've gone to the lavatory and masturbated till I'm sick of myself.' 'Cards?' I said. 'Oh, you daren't be seen playing cards,' he moaned, 'they might think you hadn't enough to do. Oh, I sit here quiet enough most times picking my nose, anyone coming past would say there's a quiet chap attending to his work watching his shaper – but my guts are tearing round inside me like torn cats to get out and do something. It's torture to look at the clock, I daren't do it. I say to myself I can bear it until tea-break, so I clench my teeth and clutch a spanner and stick it out until the hooter goes. After tea I say to myself I can bear it until dinnerbreak and so I do. I couldn't manage any other way,

I'd get stuck kicking and screaming somewhere around half-past two and never get home again.'

I sympathised with him and told him that I knew just how he felt. 'A strike is the thing,' he said, 'with pickets and punch-ups and big cheering meetings with people getting up on boxes. I do love a strike. It's three years since we had one. But I got fed up with that after a couple of days.' He looked so glum then that I thought that I should do something to cheer him up before leaving him to himself. I asked him the way to the stores and told him my concern, and as I had guessed he showed great interest. In fact he became quite enthusiastic, as if I had added a new interest to his life. 'By thunder, it would make a difference to know, wouldn't it?' he said, and took a deep breath. 'When you think of the universe, and everything cooling down to make the sun, and the earth cooling, and life happening and evolution and so on, and my father meeting my mother and me growing and then having so much trouble rearing me – and then here I am doing this, well, there doesn't seem much purpose to the Creation at all. But if I knew where my little bit went – well, I'd have a bit more respect for God.' I said that that was exactly how I felt about it, and he fell down on his knees and begged me to come back and tell me where his component went when I eventually found out. 'And yours too,' he said, getting to his feet again. 'I'd like to know.'

And so I left him very cheerful, after much handshaking, and indeed felt very cheerful myself, so that I had walked some considerable distance before I realised that he hadn't told me where to find the stores, or how to find him again afterwards, and this depressed me. It did nothing to help when I spoke to an old, old man who was leaning on a broom, and who launched immediately into a long, long story about a slotting machine. At first my interest was aroused because it was a slotting machine. I wondered if he knew that I worked in the slotting section, if he could read it in my face in some way; but eventually I decided that this was coincidence, and then I only stayed to listen because it would have been ill-mannered to go away. He was just a mad old man, obviously. He said that they (who 'they' were I could not guess) dressed this slotter up in a yellow suit and put it up on a pedestal. One of them sang to it, he said, and another went up to the canteen and fetched it three meals every day, while a third cleaned up behind it with a bucket and shovel. I kept trying to interrupt to ask him why, but he never paused, only chattered on and on. Apparently they got to fanning it with long fans and bowing down to it. The old man went into the most tedious details about how they made the fans, and the prayers they said to it, and just as I thought that manners or no I really must go, he said '...and then it spoke,' and he stopped talking. 'Spoke?' I said. 'What did it say?' The old man said that he didn't know, and as that seemed to be the end of the story I said goodbye and carried on, feeling very downhearted indeed.

It had not occurred to me that my depression might be due to lack of food, until suddenly there was a dreadful noise, absolutely unearthly, like the Devil murdering all Hell's hounds together, and I knew that it was time for midday break. Before the noise had ceased men were rushing and jostling into the gangway. Yes, I must have a meal, I told myself, and knew that at least I should have no difficulty in finding the canteen.

The machines were stopping. One man dashed round his great humped double mill like some puny referee in a heavyweight boxing match, wiping his hands and pressing buttons, while the twin cutters as big as dinner plates spun to a standstill for the first time for four hours. I followed on at the tail of the crowd, through workshops running down or already silent, and for the first time that day I felt pleasantly hungry.

I am never sure if the factory looks more like a jungle

(though I've never actually seen a jungle) or a sort of old tired museum. There is a certain amount of order, the succession of roof trusses which hold up the great sea-waves of the roof, and the vertical H girders which support them standing in long avenues down the shops; the rows of dirty enamel bowl electric lights, as high as stars in the roof. But after that there is no pattern at all, only a sort of internecine vegetable war of giant shapes and strangling ivy. Miles of inch piping, straight or bent at right-angles form a three-dimensional system of a thousand cages, conducting electrical cables to every machine and lamp, or steam or compressed air or gas to every corner. Larger pipes move more freely and less honestly about, like boa-constrictors, smothering some machines and ignoring others, sometimes arching their backs over whole shops and then swelling out into great trumpets to swallow up fire and smoke from grinders and hearths. Chains hang down everywhere, big chains some of them with links like rows of television screens, ending in dreadful hooks. Cables loop about in all directions, over and through each other, hooked up on beams, tied on to pipes with string, or just thrown over everything which happens to be in their path, and glass oil pots gleam like fruits on long stalks. Tulip lamps on broken stems bend over everything which might move, while in some shops I saw a device like a giant curtain rail threading its way up and down and round about carrying beneath it a strange jangling procession of assorted components stuck on hooks like a funeral. Heavier components were conveyed on a roller track which criss-crossed overhead in all directions exactly like a fairground switchback. Giant things resembling gas meters crouched like hunched-up gorillas in the roof beams, and everywhere there are tin boxes and cupboards all painted the same ancient green, or else completely smothered by dust. Peculiar shuttered heaters hang from the roof like vultures waiting. Amongst all this stand the machines, monsters of every possible shape, with humps and bulges and fins and towers and long moving arms, ballooning heads and hunched backs, spheres, cones and blobs ranging back into obscure dark silhouettes in the smoke. There's enough croaking and caterwauling, shrilling and gibbering and twittering for a hundred jungles; but when the machines are silent, as they were now, the place looks like a museum. The silence is like a minus sound. All movement stops, there is no more trembling. The dust settles, the lights go out. The clocks lose their gestapo character and you can hear them ticking, museum clocks with a sense of proportion, tired of time. The tall thin cupboards standing by each machine look like coffins or mummy cases; one is open to show an overcoat hanging inside it. Flat electrical switchboxes on the walls stick out of their chests like obstinate breastplates of long forgotten knights; little glass offices stand in corners – empty showcases with dusty windows. Faded charts and dirty numbers hang in rows on strings, signifying nothing. The place is uninhabited. Then the machines are stuffed whales or dinosaurs, deader than rock, with varnished skins. One might drag one's children through the place bored rigid, and they would not dare make a sound to break that silence. But soon, at one p.m. precisely, such a hell of noise will burst out suddenly from the very heaps of rubbish on the floor that you will forget what silence was, and be in the jungle again.

I scrambled up a short stairway on the heels of the last man, and burst into the canteen. Here was warmth and good humour, the bubble of voices, delicious smells, seats to sit on and food to eat. Some had started already on great platefuls of beef and roast potatoes running with blood and dark sauces. Every face was smiling, the boredom and the toil were already hours behind, the one o'clock hooter might have been weeks ahead. Cigarettes were lit as we jostled in the queue, change was jingled, jokes were told, the fat lady behind the steaming counter was teased and baited by a dozen men at once, to her obvious delight, as she sloshed and slapped around in boiling cauldrons and sizzling pans and crashed the steaming heaped-up plates down on to the counter in quick succession.

It was only after I had taken my place at the end of a table, blowing on my fingers after carrying my plate, that I realised there was some kind of concert going on, or about to take place. At one end of the canteen was an improvised stage, made up of spare tables (which looked none too strong to carry the weight of people, I thought, for the one I was sitting at was shaky enough with all the food it was carrying).

When everyone had been served the fat woman who had been serving emerged from the kitchen carrying her own meal – which you could have got into a matchbox – on a tiny white plate, and took her seat like a queen at the opposite end of my table. This seemed to be the signal for the concert to start, for a tiny little round man wearing a red coat much too long for him climbed up on to one of the tables, which creaked dangerously, and began to harangue all of us.

Sitting at the back I couldn't make out a word he was saying, but everyone else seemed to be delighted. From time to time they would all burst out laughing with their mouths full, or tip forward and blow down their noses into their plates. Somehow I couldn't just ignore him and get on with my dinner, and yet the harder I listened the less I understood. At one point when everyone shrieked with laughter one man choked and had to be taken out by two others, but the voice from the stage paused not for one second.

On and on this man talked, with people struggling to eat between convulsions of laughter, pork chops and custard pie stuck in the air in front of their mouths, but I seemed to have lost my own appetite. At length, thinking that there must be a more peaceful place than this to smoke a pipe for a while, I was about to stand up and leave when, looking along the row, I noticed that the woman at the end, the one who had served us all, was showing signs of great distress. Everyone else was so taken up with eating and watching the stage that no one had noticed her, even the man sitting next to her, and I hurried along the row as fast as I could. I reached the end of the table to find the poor woman lying on the floor, and I stepped out into the gangway and tried to lift her. But she was enormous and I couldn't have moved her, much less lifted her, so I spoke to the man who had been sitting next to her; but the man on the stage seemed to be working up to some kind of climax, the end of a joke perhaps it was, so that his audience now sat with bated breath and this man I spoke to took no notice of me. I spoke to him again. Then the woman on the floor gave a groan and twisted her body, so I dropped down to her and tried to lift, but it was no good.

I stood up and spoke to a woman on the opposite side of the gangway, but just as I did so the funny line must have come, for the audience all roared with laughter and my voice was drowned. I spoke a second time, but just then the man on the stage gave a particularly loud shout, so that again the woman didn't hear me. Again there was a loud groan from the floor, and the prostrate woman arched her back so that her huge belly reared up at me like a mountain, and it suddenly occurred to me that she was in the early stages of childbirth. I went back to the man again and took him by the shoulder and shook him, but he continued to munch away at a bone and stared in front of him. I shook him once more, very hard, and he turned on me and swore and told me to 'lay off', but before I could explain he had gone back to his bone and his staring, I shouted at him then, 'This is an emergency,' but just as I did so the whole crowd in the canteen uttered a 'Dooor!', with that deep throaty tone which one hears sometimes at a football match when somebody misses a goal, and my voice was completely drowned. I stepped quickly over the mother-to-be, who was now lying with her knees drawn up, clutching at her hips and pulling dreadful faces, back to the woman. I was sure that I should get more response from a woman, but when I got to her she and everyone else were hopping about with excitement about something which was happening on the stage, and her double chin was wobbling and her podgy little hands were clapping but not quite touching each other in a frenzy of excitement, and try as I might I could not attract her attention. I turned to a man sitting beside her and bellowed in his ear, but the audience cheered loudly, and he was shouting and took no notice. The woman on the floor was red in the face and straining, and crying out 'Oh! oh! oh!', but the man on the stage was roaring with laughter and nobody seemed to hear. Then there was dead silence. The entertainer was standing with his arms raised high in the air as if he was about to introduce the Lord Jesus Christ himself, and I saw my opportunity, drew a deep breath and bellowed as loud as I could, 'This woman is having a baby!' – but at that instant the noise of a full brass band came blaring out of the canteen loudspeaker system, that dreadful piece of music they always play at circuses, and the people in the canteen went wild and upset their cups and plates and cheered and cheered.

This was ridiculous, I said to myself, absolutely ridiculous – here am I surrounded by people, ordinary people, and I can't convey to any of them that a woman is having a baby on the floor in the middle of them. At least half-a-dozen of them could have reached out and touched her, dozens could have seen her. All at once a woman walked out on the stage. If she would recite some poetry I might be able to make someone take some notice, I thought. But immediately all the people, most of them men, of course, began to whistle through their fingers and shout out at the woman, who was doing nothing at all. They behaved like wild animals.

I drew myself up. The situation was desperate and

demanded desperate action. The woman on the floor was arching her back and gasping with pain. I fixed my eye on a timid looking man and swore a solemn oath that I would, whatever happened, if the roof were to fall in at that moment and the floor give way, rouse him to an understanding of the situation. If necessary, I told myself, I shall take him by the throat and shake the teeth from his head, such was the strength of my determination. As I stepped over the woman I shouted down to her through the clapping and pandemonium, 'Hold on, won't be long now!', but then to my horror I saw the baby's head.

What to do now? I looked at the timid man and took a step towards him. Then I looked at the baby and moved back again. Idiots or clowns were thumping about all over the stage, and the people next to me were roaring with laughter. I made as if to lunge at the man, who was banging his fists on his table with mirth, but then the woman pushed again, and I thought perhaps I should be down there holding the baby or something. It might fall on the floor or get the string thing round its neck. She strained again and I leapt down to the baby and waited. The people were so helpless with laughter now that the only way they could express their mirth was to rock from side to side together, or backwards and forwards, tearing their hair and stamping their feet. The woman pushed again, a long despairing heave so that her face turned scarlet and veins stood out on her forehead and neck. Am I supposed to pull, I asked myself? But I might hurt the baby or pull its head off even. But if I didn't pull, this woman might go on in labour for hours, and both of them die while these people laughed themselves silly a foot away. I put out my hands to the head and just then the baby came squoggling out and landed squarely in my hands. It was born!

I never reckoned that men were much moved by newborn babies. I recollected that when I first saw my own son I was astonished that so ugly a creature could be classified as human, and I hastened to ask the nurse if there was anything wrong with him. He didn't seem much better when my wife brought him home, and he displayed all sorts of disgusting habits then and I felt no love for him at all. But this little chap was altogether different, a fine podgy little man with proper features. I held him up and he opened his eyes and looked at me. He – looked – at – me. The first look that those eyes had ever taken, the first vision which had registered on the surface of a new consciousness, had been me. I was ready to fall down on my face and worship the Almighty, I wanted to stand up in that dreadful assembly and shout, 'Look, look, you bloody fools, while you've been acting the goat and stuffing your stinking faces into your pigtroughs a miracle has happened, a pure shining blasted miracle!' I felt so proud I might have been the father himself; no, better than the father, where was he now? He might be at work, at work here, he might be in the canteen, he might be this man here with tears running down his dirty face and gravy all over his chin. No, I wasn't the father, I was the midwife. But midwives deliver a dozen babies a day and think nothing of it. This baby was special, unique, this baby was the only baby in the world, the only free, innocent, decent, honest human being in the whole bloody universe, and I was the Lord God Almighty himself holding him in my hands. His hands were like my hands down to the last tiniest fingernail, his feet had five toes, and there was his little penis all tiny and wrinkled, just like they are in those paintings ...

Then I caught sight of the cord thing, a long red wriggly thing attached at one end to the baby and at the other to the mother. Was he not really born yet then? I gave the cord a little tug, and more of it came out of the mother, like string out of a dispenser. I seemed to remember that it had to be cut – no, the ends tied in a knot before it was cut. But how could I tie the ends before I had cut them? I thought back to my scout days. No, it was technically impossible to tie more than one knot in it before it was cut. Then which side of the knot should I cut? If I cut the baby's side, the baby would die – if I cut the mother's side then she might die. I was ignorant. I looked in desperation down the rows of shouting people. They were drumming now, drumming and stamping in dreadful unison, each one with a knife in his right hand and a fork in his left hand, banging them down alternately on the tables, making the cruets jump and the plates rattle and all shouting together as they did so '– knife, fork, knife, fork, knife, fork –' so loud that my ears were hurting me. I stood up then and held the baby high up above my head and screamed 'For God's sake help me!'. But the chant only grew louder. Images were flicking through my mind. I saw the cinema at home full of children, 'Saturday Morning Club' it was called, and the place packed out with children bellowing out a particular line of the Club Song which we sang every week before the show began – 'We are ten thousand strong, how can we all be wrong! We are ten thousand strong, how can we all be wrong!'

I looked at the baby. He was changing colour to a bluish shade and his eyes had closed. '– knife, fork, knife, fork, knife, fork, knife, fork –' Now a man had come on the stage and started to appeal for silence, but it did not come. He raised his hands for a while, and then he straightened his jacket and tried again with his arms raised. No effect, so he dusted his trousers down and pressed his hands together in front of him and looked at his shoes, while the chant went on, '– knife, fork, knife, fork –' Of course, the baby hadn't cried! The thought struck me like a bucket of cold water. Tickle his feet. I did and nothing happened. The man had his hands up again and I suddenly realised that he was appealing for silence on my behalf. This time the noise did begin to subside. I held the baby upside down and shook it, and listened for its breathing. There was nothing. I slapped it on the back, pinched its buttocks, bellowed, 'Cry!' into its ear and rubbed its chest frantically. But after all that I was left with a limp blue thing like a skinned rabbit. The baby was dead.

There was silence now. As the man walked down between the tables towards me everyone turned to stare at me. I held the baby out awkwardly and when the man took it from me I walked straight to the door without saying anything or looking back. As I went down the stairs I heard bedlam break out again up there, and someone shouted angrily, 'He let it die, the bloody murderer!', and a woman crying.

chapter five

Down in the factory they seemed already to have started. I leant forward into the sound and pushed, as one does against a wind. All around me metal was raging and hurling itself round in circles because it could not hurl itself at me, and the men looked as if they were all seized with convulsions. I could not go on because I was lost, and every attempt to ask the way was either unsuccessful or resulted in long delay, and sometimes even unpleasantness. I couldn't go back to the slotting section for the same reason. But just as my mood was blackest I thought that I had found the place.

Ahead of me a large area was divided off, with steel sheeting, mesh and angle-iron forming a barrier ten feet or so in height topped with three strands of barbed wire. I reached the barrier and scanned its length for a door, but none was visible. The steel sheeting which formed the bottom part of the wall was just too high for me to look over, so I walked the two hundred yards or so to the next corner of the enclosure and looked along the other wall, but there seemed to be no entrance in that either. However, I could see a sort of hatchway about halfway down, where the steel sheeting was no higher than shoulder level, so I walked down and peeped in.

A man was standing just inside who at first sight appeared to have two heads, one growing out of the top of the other. Both of the heads looked at me in astonishment and the man turned sideways quickly to pick up something. I saw then there were in fact two men, one a tiny dwarf sitting on the shoulders of the other and clutching him round the neck so that he couldn't move his head. They swivelled back to face me, the taller man brandishing a large spanner in a threatening way, as if he expected me to attack him. How he thought I could do so from the other side of all this steel mesh I did not know, but I spoke to him politely to put him at ease. 'Good afternoon,' I said. 'Please excuse me, but could you tell me if this is the General Parts Stores?' 'No,' whispered the dwarf, and 'No!' repeated the man with the spanner. 'This is the toolroom,' murmured the dwarf, which the other also repeated in a loud voice. 'Ask him if he wants to come in,' whispered the dwarf. 'Do you want to come in?' demanded the man, brandishing the spanner. 'Why no,' I answered, 'I am looking for the General Parts Stores.' 'Then he does want to come in,' hissed the dwarf, and the other man braced himself as if he thought I was about to crash through the barrier. I assured them that I did not want to come into the toolroom, but the dwarf told me that I most certainly did because it was the only way to get to the stores. They then debated whether they should let me in, in whispers so that I couldn't understand any of it. 'Ask him what he does,' whispered the dwarf. The other did, and when I told them they debated some more. 'All right then,' the big man said, 'but be careful and keep yourself to yourself. If anyone asks you what you're doing in here tell them that you are only passing through to get to the stores.'

I said that I had no objection to that, and after the dwarf had added that I mustn't on any account touch anything or ask anyone what they were doing, the big man began to draw bolts and take off padlocks on the other side of the barrier. Presently a small section of the sheeting slid aside and they told me to step through. I did so, and then he put the sheeting back and secured it again with great care, checking each device many times over.

I saw that the whole enclosure was itself divided up into

small enclosures, each one not much bigger than a small room. 'Come this way,' said the big man, and I followed to a door, which he began to unlock. 'This place seems to be well guarded,' I said, to make conversation. The man stopped what he was doing, and they both looked at me. 'Yes,' said the big man, 'we have a lot to guard.' 'Oh?' I said. The dwarf whispered something, and the other repeated, 'Pride of tradition.' 'Traditional superiority,' whispered the dwarf, and the man repeated this also. 'Pride of workmanship,' they both said. I looked around. Apart from all the barriers things looked exactly the same in here as outside. There were the same machines all crammed in together, and the men were indistinguishable from those in the other shops, and they all looked just as vacant and just as bored.

They unlocked the door and let me through, locked it again and escorted me across a room full of a variety of machines, the operators of which stared at me in a hostile way. Through another door and across another section identical with the last, then through another tediously locked door. At each door the big man produced a great clump of keys like a large bunch of mistletoe, and sorted through them for a full minute at each lock, with the dwarf reaching down over his head and turning them about. Since every door had at least three locks, our progress was slow.

As I was waiting to go through yet another door I noticed that in the next section a crowd of men were standing and pissing up into the air. When one had finished another stepped forward and did the same and so it went on. I turned to my two-tiered guide and asked for an explanation. 'Can't they get out to go to the proper place?' I said. The big man pushed open the door and I stepped through. 'They are,' said the dwarf, 'deciding who is the best man among them.' I said that I thought there were better ways of deciding who was the best man. We set out across another section, full of machines. 'Surely,' I said, 'to take a tape measure and find out who was the tallest would be better than that.' The dwarf said that they had thought of that, but that all the short men objected although the tall men, so he said, had assured the short men that they had an equal chance of winning. 'What happened then?' I asked. 'Well, the short men suggested that everyone should be weighed in turn,' said the dwarf, 'because, they said, obviously whoever weighed the least was the best man, but the tall men all said that that wasn't fair. The short men said that everyone would be weighed on the same scales with the same weights and so of course it was fair, and that the tall men were just being awkward, but they dropped that idea in the end.'

I asked him what happened then, and he said that the tall men had proposed that it should be decided by finding out who could run fastest. He said that when the short men objected to that the tall men told them not to be so unsportsmanlike, and they should let the best man win and so forth. 'And then,' said the dwarf, 'a man with a long nose proposed that they should measure their noses, and choose the man with the longest, and a man who had only one eye kept shouting "The one-eyed man is best", but nobody took any notice of him.' 'Surely,' I said, as we reached another door, 'if it is so difficult to decide, then obviously the men must all be so good that there is little to choose between them. Is it so vital to find out who is best?'

The two of them stopped in the middle of sorting for the key and looked at me in shocked amazement. 'Are you suggesting,' said the dwarf, 'that they might be all equal?' I hastily assured them that I certainly did not. 'But,' I added, 'may they not be all very nearly equal?' 'Then it is even more important,' snapped the dwarf, 'to find out who is the best.' They turned back to the keys. 'The winner,' said the dwarf, as he turned the keys over one by one, 'is to be dressed up in a yellow top hat and purple robes, and carried at the head of a procession throughout the length and breadth of the factory for everyone to see.' 'I see,' I said as the door opened. 'Yes,' said the dwarf, quite unpleasantly, as we stepped through and closed the door behind us. 'You don't seriously think that someone like yourself, for instance, would ever be carried shoulder high in a procession through the factory like that, do you?' 'Good heavens,' I said, 'certainly not.'

At this point the dwarf said that they had a little matter to attend to, and would I mind waiting there a short while? I said of course not, and they disappeared through another door. I never saw them again.

After a great length of time I walked over to the opposite door and peeped through it. In the next section there was nothing but a large facing-table, the largest and heaviest I had ever seen, and a great stack of components in one corner, obviously waiting to be inspected on the table. Around the latter was a crowd of coloured West Indians playing a furious game of dominoes. I could tell that they were West Indians by the clothes they wore – green and yellow trilbies and brightly coloured shirts not tucked into their trouser-tops. They were playing dominoes in a way which more resembled hand-to-hand warfare than that gentle pastime of the English public house. Each man played his piece by lifting it above his head and slamming it down on to the table with all his strength, so that the metal table rang like a bell, and then the whole group would roar with laughter and clap each other on the back, until the next man's piece would set them all craning their necks to see. At one point they all threw their hands in the air and staggered off in mock astonishment or horror to the very corners of the room, and I thought that they had finished the game; but they immediately all rushed back to see what the next piece would be, and carried on. So violently did they play that in each move the pieces already on the table were scattered in confusion, some falling on to the floor, even; but the players didn't seem at all bothered and nobody attempted to replace the pieces, so I presumed that each man kept a record of the game in his head, as blind men play chess without a board. Looking closer I saw that all the dominoes were more or less blank, for the spots had been chipped or worn away by many violent games.

One of the men spotted me, and, smiling broadly as if I was an old friend, strode over to the door and pulled it open, although I was certain that it had been locked. 'Come in, man,' he shouted, as if I was three shops away. 'My name's Hartlepool, James Jesus Cranborough Hartlepool,' and he grasped my hand and shook it, pulling me through the door. I told him my name, which seemed to be important, and then I had to shake hands with all of them in turn, each man transferring his row of dominoes from his right hand to his left and back again to do so. 'Do you play, man?' I said that I didn't, and asked them how it was that they had so much free time, for I could see that the table was polished silver by their playing. 'Nothin' to do, Pinqu'n man,' said one, as they resumed play. 'We came here hoping for some piecework, but they told us we'd have to be labourers, and we've been stuck in here with nothin' to do ever since we got off the boat.'

We chatted about this and that, and finally I told Hartlepool the position. 'Dwarf?' he said finally. 'I never seen no dwarf,' but then he said that he knew where the stores was. 'A yellow door,' he said, 'I know about a yellow door. Nobody ever used it while I been here, but I do remember that there is a yellow door, man.'

We left the others crashing away at the dominoes, and walked over to the heap of castings in one corner. On the other side of it was a sort of corridor and Hartlepool led the way down it, muttering about the yellow door. 'I've never known anyone to come this way, I'm truly certain sure – but I did hear tell of a door ...'

We walked for some time down the corridor, and the air grew colder and the light grew dimmer, and I began to doubt if this was really the way, for surely the stores would be more accessible and more frequently used. I said as much to Hartlepool, but he said that this was almost certainly the back way to the stores. Then he stopped and pointed in front of him.

Peering past him I saw what looked like a heap of clothes and shoes piled up against the wall, but when we went closer we found to our amazement that it was a pile of human bodies, which all but concealed a yellow door. They were packed so tightly up against it that when my companion tried to drag away one of the bodies by its feet he found it impossible to move.

'Perhaps after all I won't bother about the door,' I said, and began to hurry away, but the coloured man had begun to pull at the feet with great enthusiasm and cried, 'Give us a hand here, man,' so that I felt that I had to go back to him at least. At length he dragged out the body of an old man, whose teeth were still clenched tightly on to a piece of clothing material from inside the heap. He looked balefully up at us like someone who has been disturbed from sleep to be reminded of some tiresome duty, and he looked fidgety and worried even in death. Hartlepool heaved at one or two more feet, but the bodies were so twined about with each other and so tightly packed against the door that he couldn't move any more. 'Please don't bother,' I said, but he scuttled off back down the corridor and disappeared, to return, almost before I had begun to follow him, with all the rest of the West Indians, all craning their necks and showing the whites of their eyes in the gloom, and jabbering, 'Look at all them jumbies, man!' with enthusiastic awe. Hartlepool brought up the rear with a pair of huge tongs over his shoulder and immediately they set to with the tongs, sinking them into a leg and forming a tug o' war team, each man holding the waist of the man in front. Out came a body, like a dead worm, with his jacket all up over his head and arms trailing. With a cheer they applied the tongs again and brought out a man clutching a baby's feeding-bottle in his hand. One man said something about spaghetti which the others thought uproariously funny, and laughed and made slurping noises with their mouths. All this I thought very distasteful. Some of the bodies had fouled themselves considerably, but this seemed not to bother the labourers at all, and when one huge body which they were dragging out by the head refused to budge any further, they dropped the tongs and set to work disentangling the arms and legs by hand, singing and whistling current popular tunes. I imagined that they were glad of something to do after so many hours of dominoes, but such good humour in the presence of the dead seemed to me to be indelicate.

Soon the heap was cleared away and the door exposed. Yellow it was, but its paint was all scratched and knocked about, and parts of the door had been split by heavy blows, while one little man, who had big splinters of wood clamped between his teeth, seemed to have chewed almost through in one place. The door-knob was missing and the door did not yield to pushing, so one of the labourers made a half-hearted attempt to pick the lock with the tongs, which was impossible because they were much too big. I would have told them not to bother, but I was afraid that they might be offended, having gone to so much trouble already.

I gave the door one or two desultory thumps with my fist, then a great heavy man as black as pitch stepped up, grasped me round the waist, and suggested that we put our shoulders to the door together. Before I could protest he ran at the door dragging me with him, and together we hit it with great force, which winded me but did nothing to the door. The man traggled back again several yards, still holding me around the waist, and asked two of the others to bind with us for another try. Two stepped forward and another arm went round my waist like a chainwrench, then I was bundled into the door again with even greater force. I protested that I didn't wish to put them to all this trouble, but they said, far from being a trouble it was the happiest pleasure, and I was once again trundled up against the door.

The West Indians showed tremendous good humour at all this, and flashed their teeth about and laughed unintelligible things to each other and slapped each other about and soon I was being battered against the door with the whole crowd of them behind me. Each time we arrived at the door they all feigned in various ways the pain and discomfort I actually felt, throwing up their hands in the air and shouting 'Lord Jesus man save us' and collapsing in a heap, then all rolling around on the floor helpless with laughter, with their eyes all creased up to slits and their great white teeth waving about. Some imitated briefly the attitudes of the dead people who lay about nearby, to the almost epileptic mirth of their companions, who wrung their hands and shook their heads in a laughter which rendered them incapable of making any further noise or any other gesture. Then they would pick up their hats, still wide-mouthed with mirth, and after leaning on each other a little would gather round me as if I were the master of ceremonies, and all drunken and tearful with laughter manoeuvre me back again.

So much good humour was unnatural I thought, as we rushed towards the door for what must have been the twelfth time, and, thus variously preoccupied with the means rather than the end, we were all taken completely by surprise when the door yielded and sent us sprawling through like a slot-machine jackpot. Instantly I was blinded by a tremendous light and by a terrible wind. Screwing up my eyes in pain I realised that we were outside, in the open air, in the sunlight, exposed to all the elements. I turned around on all fours as quickly as I could and groped about for the doorway.

A gruff voice from somewhere behind me, sounding echoless and naked in the air, said, 'Where d'ya think you're going?' 'I am trying to get in again,' I said, and added, 'I should be grateful to you if you could tell me where the door is, since you seem to be able to see in this dreadful light.' 'It's only the sunlight,' said the voice apologetically. 'Are you not used to it?' I told him that I left my home at seven a.m. every morning and seldom returned there before six in the evening. 'I have not seen my own garden by daylight for two months, and I shall not see the sun until March.' 'You exaggerate, surely,' said the voice. 'Work it out for yourself, then,' I said impatiently. 'Meanwhile, would you please tell me which way I have to turn to find the doorway in the wall?' 'Have you got a permit from your foreman to leave the works premises?' said the voice. 'I do not wish to leave them,' I replied, groping about the wall, my teeth chattering in the wind, 'I wish to do the opposite.' 'In that case, then,' said the voice, 'I shall have to classify you as officially late. No employee may enter the works premises after 8.15 a.m. without being classified as officially late and being put in my little book. Name and number, please.'

I was beginning to feel a headache coming on with all this light and wind. This, I thought, must be what it feels like to be one of those little grey insects which live under trunks and old linoleum, and hurry off to get away from light when they are uncovered as if it were scorching their backs. I remembered a game we used to play as children with maggots and a torch, whenever we could find the maggots and steal a torch. 'Surely there's no need to be so official,' I said. 'I only wish to know, as one man to another, and as briefly as possible, where is the doorway. I shall then enter it, and you will never see me again.' 'Officially,' he said, in a high, impersonal, official kind of tone, as if I had just called him by his schoolboy nickname, 'officially, moreover, there is no door there.'

At this point I found the door, which had closed itself. I could find no handle, but I dug my fingers in around the edges. 'Oh, it's all right,' I shouted over my shoulder. 'I've found it, thanks.' The voice bellowed back angrily, 'Nonsense!' and I heard a shrill whistle, and shouts from further away. The door seemed to be jammed. I tugged harder, still screwing up my eyes against the light. The wind was blowing up my trouserlegs and down my sleeves, and my overall jacket slapped about quite painfully. Several times more the voice roared out, 'Nonsense, nonsense,' and then I heard the barking and baying of great dogs, and a noise like the cracking of whips. Again I tugged. The voice was ranting on, saying something else which I couldn't understand, but very angry, and then there was a slapping noise like several dozen heavy books falling on the ground, then a curse and another whistle. I pulled again, as hard as I could, and the door opened. I stepped through to the sound of heavy running footsteps coming towards me, and the harsh panting of dogs straining in collars. I pulled the door to in the warmth and shade of the factory, and waited, for I was quite willing to give my name and number. I had only wanted to get out of the cold and the sunlight. But there was no sound, not so much as a knock from the door. I turned and walked away from it, wondering if I could have imagined all those voices and noises. I had seen nothing. Perhaps it was just the wind, I thought; that was it, just the wind and the sun. I must remember to take care to cover my head on holiday this year, I thought, as I looked around to see which way I should go.

It suddenly struck me that I was no longer in the toolroom, there were no barriers or partitions to be seen anywhere. I was puzzled, but I also felt a sense of relief. I was standing between two towering machines which looked like giant spiders mounted on huge pedestals. Down from the bodies of the spiders, in the centre of the splayed steel legs which were as thick as my arm, hung a bunch of long tools, each one mounted on a shining vertical slide. These tools were plunged down into the throats of six steel cylinders which were mounted in a circle. Each cylinder revolved slowly, and presently the tools all withdrew up into the body of the spider and the circle of cylinders moved round so that each cylinder took up the place previously occupied by its neighbour. The tools then moved down into the rotating cylinders as before, and the great spider resumed its meditation. Alternately the two machines sent the cylinders about their solemn dance, together they carried on their business like the engines of Fate. There were no operators in attendance on either machine. Surely someone must reload these machines when they had completed their components, I thought. But there was nobody, so I walked on to the next machine.

This was a tremendous multiple spindled drill. I had never been so close to one of these machines before. The huge motor was mounted on top of a tall square steel tower, upon the side of which hung the great hood containing the spindles. There were many dozens of these, so that looking into the hood through one of its windows was like peering through the stalks of a bed of giant reeds, not all vertical but criss-crossing about to drive the drills wherever they were positioned. The drills all hung down below the hood like a mass of spiral stalactites, some large like hunks of fat new rope, some fine as hairs, all in an upside down fantastic forest or turning polished spirals, where you might hunt the upside down unicorn with sharpened barbers' poles, or find whirlwinds growing like toadstools in the corkscrew grass.

The amazing thing about the machine was the number of people who seemed to be working it, or with it. There was an operator who ran about ceaselessly, attending to buttons and wheels and levers as the great hood slid slowly down the pillar with the ease of a balloon, the drills beneath it all drilling down furiously through the air. The little man skipped and hustled through the monkey-puzzle of knobs and levers, then paused briefly to watch the drills enter the jig. They dived into their respective holes, all screeching and scratching suddenly with unpleasant metally mice noises. They were through the jig and into the component without a pause, a horde of squirming maggots, scoring and boring and throwing out shavings, the smaller drills in busy little spurts, the larger ones in slow pulses like the pumping of a heart. A crack, and the hood moved upwards, dragging the drills wriggling up and away by their tails, up the pillar with unnatural grace, like a haughty prestidigitating rat-catcher, while the second man, a great over-muscled one-eyed fellow in a dirty overall, stepped forward to help the first drag out the heavy component from the jig. They put it down on the floor and turned to pick up another, whereupon it was pounded on by a little man wearing a leather apron, who furiously scraped and scratched and filed about all over it. When he had finished it with a wipe of a dirty rag and a blow or two, he was elbowed aside by another man in a grey overall coat who applied all kinds of strange gadgets to it in various places. After a few seconds he withdrew with his armful of gadgets to make way for a long thin spectacled man in a white coat who took various measurements with a ruler and a micrometer and a little gauge, before turning to consult with the gadget man. After a few seconds the two of them moved over to a triangular man in a pink coat and spoke to him, whereupon he selected with a flourish a small punch from a box, took a hammer in his other hand, bent over the component and stamped it soundly on one corner. Then another man in a white coat with a large note-pad and bulldog clip under his arm bent down and peered about all round the component and stepped back to make notes while two labourers came forward, picked it up and heaved it up on to the top of a pile of its fellows.

While all this was happening the actual operator of the drill had drilled two more components, and was now rushing round preparing for the third. When it had been lifted into the jig I went forward to the atlas man, intending to ask him the way to the stores, but before I could speak he swivelled his one eye all over me, put an arm lightly about my shoulders and pointed to a disc of light which quivered on the side of the machine. 'The sun,' he said. 'Through the roof he comes and swings across the workshop like the moving fingerprint of fate.' 'Really?' I said. 'At eight he comes down out of that corner up there and slides across the clock face, then he skips over those heating pipes and jumps across the three girders, creeps across the top of the Cincinatti, down the middle of the grinder and on to this machine. Sometimes he comes on to my head when I'm not looking, warm and soft like a mother's hand. Then he creeps across the floor and up the gangway, whipping up the dust and drinking the tea. He's away up by the foreman's office by five. I always say goodnight to him, but some spit on him.' He made a gesture in the direction of the disc. 'Look how he trembles and dances, like those hoverflies that hang by the walls on hot summer days. If you watch you can see the clouds go across his face, clear as clear, like television, and sometimes you can see leaves and even birds, all upside down. Excuse me.' He stepped forward to help with another component.

When he came back I asked him if he could tell me the way to the General Parts Stores, and he immediately said, 'Yes, carry straight on and you'll come to it.' I asked him if that was all and he said yes, that was all; so I walked on. Presently I came to a door and went through, and found myself in a long dark hall which seemed to be some kind of laboratory, for it was full of boxes and cages of various kinds, some looking like large hen-batteries, some like rabbit hutches. I could not decide whether these cages contained any animals, or indeed anything at all, because there wasn't enough light, and since it was quite cold in the hall, and there seemed to be no human beings about, I thought there was nothing to be gained by dawdling about to examine the cages. Again I heard that strange booming noise far above my head, as if the roof were being lifted by a great wind, but it was too dark to see clearly. All the roof glass seemed to have been painted with a dark green wash to keep out the light, or perhaps some dense creeper was growing over the outside of the glass – I could not tell. I hurried on.

Presently, on looking up, I saw a vague white shape over to my right, which seemed to be hurrying to intercept me at a point ahead where I could see that several gangways intersected. What could this man, if it was a man – well, of course it was a man – want with me? I walked faster. If the stores lay immediately ahead, as the one-eyed man had said, then what need had I to speak to anyone else? Ahead of me I could just make out what looked like the far door of the hall. In half a minute I could be out again into the lighted workshops, or into the stores even; why should I be forced to meet this figure? I was only passing through, I had touched nothing, looked at nothing. If people weren't supposed to pass through, then why was there a gangway, with a door at each end? The door I had come in by wasn't locked, in fact it was wide open. There were no notices.

As our paths converged I saw that the figure was slightly ahead of me. I began to walk very fast indeed, while at the same time trying not to give the impression that I was hurrying. But the figure still kept just ahead. A group of large containers passed between us, and when the figure emerged from the other side we were quite close to each other. I looked across at him, while at the same time trying to give the impression that I was looking straight ahead, and saw that he carried a length of stout rope. All sorts of ridiculous ideas went through my head then, but I said to myself that all things had a rational explanation and I had nothing to fear.

I arrived at the junction, which was only a few yards from the far door, to find my way barred by a desperate looking man in a long white coat, who was extending towards me a length of rope tied at one end with a noose. 'Good afternoon,' I said, and he then told me that he was about to hang himself, and would I please do him the service of swinging on his legs?

I expressed astonishment, and then disapproval. I said that I certainly would not swing on his legs, that furthermore I considered it my duty to do everything in my power to prevent him from hanging himself. He burst into tears at this and said that there was no one left in the world with any consideration for individual wishes. 'If I have decided to do this because of my circumstances, who are you to come interfering when you know nothing of them?' I said I was sorry and that perhaps if he told me all about it I might be better able to judge his intention. (Secretly I thought that if he unburdened himself to me he might feel a great deal better and throw away the rope.)

'When I was young,' he said, 'I was very romantic, and set out on a quest for the perfect woman. I knew exactly what she must be like and carried blueprints of her in my pocket, together with exact details of the answers she would give to a large number of questions on various matters such as foreign affairs, philosophy, religion, sex and so on, but mostly sex. I roamed all the countryside and towns of England in search of her, and lived among nobility and among whores. I searched the churches and the schools, the dance halls and the cinemas, and went from house to house knocking on the doors and showing my blueprint. At last I found her, with her heel jammed in a moving staircase in a London underground, and I rescued her and we fell in love.

'We couldn't get married because at that time we hadn't enough money and couldn't find an empty house anywhere, so we both worked hard and saved and spent our free time just looking at each other in wonderful anticipation. Her body was as round and sound as a fresh ripe melon and mine as hard and strong as steel cables and we used to sit and stroke one another and dream about what it would be like when we were married. I used to tell her how I'd slap her bum and chase her up and down the stairs and around the tables and chairs, and she used to say how she'd squeal and throw away her clothes one by one, and lock herself in the bathroom and put scent and powder all over herself while I scaled up the drainpipe after her. And I told her how I'd stride through the streets at night holding her with her legs wrapped round me, showing her to policemen, and bouncing along the high street with dogs barking, lights going on and people opening windows to see what the commotion was about. And she used to describe how she'd never let go and make me walk round the house so that she could get all the cooking and cleaning done without having to separate, and then I'd tell her how we'd run over the roofs and chimney pots and fences and through the back gardens and chase across the fields and through woods and over the haystacks and hedges to places where the ferns would tickle her breasts and scratch her back and no one would see but the sun and the moon, to rise and set and rise and set and always be ready to start all over again in the morning.'

'Good heavens,' I said.

'Yes, and we used to work each other up in a terrible state like that, and feel quite ill, but we always said we'd wait however long it took, because all the books said it was the right thing to do. We used to go out every day and look for houses with nobody in them, and then we'd find one and move in all the furniture, and be all dressed up at the church and just going to put the ring on when someone would come running up telling us we'd no business to move in there because it was due to be pulled down or something.

'So back we'd go and work some more and I'd say to her, never mind. I'll put you under my arm and get an axe and go up into the woods and cut down trees, and hack out notches at the end so they fit together and sweat and strain night and day until I've built a house and she'd say yes, I'll lay you on the grass and bring you water and bathe your hands every day, and lie beside you and rub your arms new again every night. Then I'd say, we'll buy the Karma Sutra and learn it off by heart and when we've gone right through it we'll start at the beginning again, and I said I'd cover the walls with pictures of her, and kiss every one every day and put new ones up every week.'

He burst out crying and put the noose over his head, so I pressed him to go on, hoping that it would help. 'Well then, one windy day after we'd been waiting fifteen years I chased a councillor's hat, and so we got a council house. But it wasn't like we'd planned at all. All there ever was was a bit of jumping around on the bed, and in the morning we sat up and looked at each other and wondered what it was all about. We tried it once in a field but we got too cold and then it rained.' 'But the sexual act,' I said to him, determined to change his mind, 'is the utmost sacred expression of love between man and woman.'

He smiled a sad smile and the noose around his neck lent him a kind of dignity, of fearless martyrs or doomed generals. 'The sexual act,' he replied, 'may be an expression of anything you like. It may be an expression of the desire to dominate or to submit; of the desire to cause or to experience pain; it may be a form of argument, a form of escape, a form of blackmail; it may be punishment, penance, habit or just like going to the lavatory. In our minds it had built itself up week by week like a cathedral behind a curtain. It grew and grew in size and splendour until towards the end we fancied that it must be built of solid gold. When the curtain finally went up there was nothing but a few flowers, and charging about like bulls I suppose we must have trampled on them all. I realised that all women are fundamentally just as white and floppy and repulsive as my grandmother, whom I saw naked by accident when I was five, and was ill for a week after. They're no less sweaty and smelly to share a bed with than men, really. Two people in the same bed is something we should have given up at the same time as we invented drains and flush lavatories.'

He grimaced and climbed up on a box holding the end of the rope in his hand. 'There's more to marriage than that, surely,' I called to him. 'There certainly is,' he said, almost without stopping for breath. 'There's an earthquake when the milk boils and a world crisis if the bathwater isn't hot, blue-black screaming bloody revolution if the groceries aren't delivered on the right day, and absolute prostrated end of the world if the nappies aren't properly aired. There's rows if I walk in in dirty shoes, rows if I don't sit down to meals she cooks for me. They say that you say things in a row that you don't mean, but it isn't true. The horror of it is that you say things that you do mean, and mean all the time but won't face up to.' He tested the noose. 'If I'm half-an-hour late getting back from work I find her screaming and shouting about the house with all the taps turned on and all the doors and windows open that I'm run over in the road, dead and buried. If I stayed away for a whole night she'd have murdered the children and herself as well by morning.'

'I know just how it is,' I said in what I hoped was a comforting sort of way. 'We just have to learn to live with these little things, that's all.' Then he looped the free end of the rope over a dangling crane-hook, and glared down at me. 'I don't wish to live with them,' he said. 'Think of your children,' I suggested. 'I do, I do,' he returned, adjusting the noose on his neck. 'You know, I used to hate those child murderers you read about in the papers who get three months. I used to hate them along with everyone else, but now I understand. Nothing on earth so persistently asks to be murdered as your own children, and when they howl she howls too, when she howls they scream, when they scream she shouts at me, and when she shouts at me they kick me and punch me and she pulls their hair and I get to shouting at all of them. It's like living with all the devils in bedlam. Sometimes we have a quiet weekend and then we look back on it like a month's holiday and say, do you remember that quiet weekend we had last year? But it's not enough to live on.' He made as if to jump, and in desperation I shouted, 'Well, there's your work then!' but then he did jump, and the bones of his neck clicked like castanets and he was dead before I could do anything.

What now? Does one phone for a doctor? There was no phone, and what good could a doctor do? Must I go and find someone and say, 'A man just hung himself while I was talking to him?' There would be awkward questions, and even more delay. I resolved to say nothing to anyone and walked out of the hall.

Once through the door and the episode might have been a trick of the imagination, for here I was back in a workshop, walking between the noisy machines. I was quite certain that the stores were very close now, so that when a man I spoke to offered to show me to the door I followed him, and was completely bewildered when he pushed me into a tiny room, the walls of which were entirely covered with pornographic photographs. There was an almost life-size picture of a naked girl leaping out of the sea like a prize salmon, her hair (which was perfectly dry) flying in the sunlight. There was a picture of another girl playing an accordion, which was just large enough for her to give an impression of attempting to preserve her modesty, but not quite enough for her to be completely successful. Photographs there were of what looked like naked wet-nurses thrusting forward enormous breasts like headlamps as if their lives depended on them, while others put forward for examination their buttocks or their bellies. Others stretched on beds and paid court to lethargic hairy dogs; one completely naked young woman seemed to have been photographed in a crowded street, smiling at a man using a road-drill. A pink woman in a ridiculously short transparent pink nightdress was stooping to light two large red candles. There was not a square inch of the wall which did not display some piece of bulging female body, and the effect of so much concentrated anatomical detail was to give an impression of something medical or scientific rather than sexual.

I was bewildered. I turned to the man but did not know whether to express disgust or indifference, or congratulate him, or ask him what he meant by showing me in here when I had asked for the stores, or simply tell him politely that I did not think this was the stores. Eventually I said, 'Thank you,' and hurried away. A little further on I asked again for the stores, but was shown into a deserted cloakroom by a man who did not speak. I took my leave of him and when I was out of his sight (for I did not wish to offend him) asked again, but by three different men in succession I was shown a disused boiler room, a bay where stacker trucks were stored when not in use and a sand-blasting unit. Each one assured me that what he was showing me was the General Parts Stores and told me to enter and wait until somebody came, although the last would have been extremely dangerous to enter. I hurried away completely bewildered, reflecting that not only did these people not know where the stores was; they also did not know what it was. I was despairing of ever finding the place when another man assured me that there was no such place as the General Parts Stores.

Completely discouraged then, I told him my whole problem, and he immediately declared that I needed to find not the stores, but the assembly line. He explained this to me in some detail, and I became convinced that he was right. 'After all,' he said, and this sounded very reasonable, 'there you will find your pulley being assembled into its proper place, and if you follow it along the line you will eventually see it in action.' I thanked him very sincerely, and asked him how I could get to the assembly line. 'There, I confess, I cannot be of help,' he said, 'but if you walk on you will certainly find someone somewhere who knows.'

I trudged on. I was tired, and for some time another matter had been bothering me. But by luck I chanced on a notice saying 'Gentlemen', and opened the door. I was a little apprehensive because of the strange episode which had taken place in the last lavatory I had been in, but once inside this one my fears vanished. This was a neat, tidy and clean lavatory. Everything shone, and there was a clean sort of smell. There were only five cubicles, for it was a very small lavatory. The place was deserted. I pushed open the middle door and shortly took my seat on a very comfortable pedestal. There was even toilet paper provided in a china dispenser which had little flowers on it, and this was remarkable.

Presently I heard several men come in through the door and then there were voices and the rattle and hiss of matches. The fragrant smoke of tobacco drifted under the door. They were standing just outside my cubicle, and as the door did not come down to the ground, but stopped a good foot above it, I could see their shoes and boots. There was a pair of clogs, I noticed, and many pairs of huge boots, dusty and hobnailed. A pair of Wellingtons flip-flopped about, and a shiny pair of brown shoes stood one on top of the other for some reason.

As I contemplated these I heard a scuffling beside me. The partitions between the cubicles did not go all the way down to the floor either, and I looked down to see the back of a head which was coming through from the cubicle on my right. It was followed quickly by shoulders, arms, torso and all of a long thin man in an overall coat who stood up in front of me and brushed himself down quickly. He had his back to me, and although the cubicle was scarcely big enough to hold two of us he seemed not to see me at all, and unbolted the door of my cubicle and let himself out. I pushed the door to, of course; and as he was a thin man it hadn't opened far enough to give anybody any cause for embarrassment. But I felt peculiarly upset, and it occurred to me that if I were to leave this cubicle now it would seem very strange to the men outside, who would have no alternative but to believe that I had just taken part in some unnatural activity. I was dismayed by this. I bolted the door quietly, replaced my trousers and waited for some time. But the boots showed no signs of moving. I hadn't time to waste like this, and hit upon the idea of crawling under a partition myself. But should I crawl to the left or to the right? My brief visitor had come from the right – therefore, I thought, the right-hand cubicle would be more likely than the cubicle to my left to be both empty and locked, thus saving risk of further embarrassment.

I went down on my hands and knees and started to squeeze underneath the partition, but I was stouter than the other man had been and had a good deal of difficulty. The cubicle, however, was both empty and locked, and this gave me encouragement and I gladly suffered a bruise or two. After brushing myself down I unbolted the door and made as if to stride out confidently, but I was amazed to find a crowd of burly men all round the door waiting for me. They dragged me out and pushed me about and told me that I was disgusting, and what did I mean to do about it? I said that it obviously wasn't me at all but the man who had just left the next cubicle, and that I had only that moment crawled under the partition of this cubicle from the next door. They all laughed then, and one said he thought at least I had had time to think up something better than that while I was in there. 'Why didn't you crawl out, then?' shouted one. 'The other man did that,' I tried to explain, but they hooted with laughter and grabbed me and lifted me up on to their shoulders. Then they carried me out of the lavatory, all together in a crowd, out into the factory, shouting to people to come and see. They marched along the main gangway between the machines, holding me up above them and shouting, 'Look, look, at last we've caught him, at last, at last!' Men looked up, or shouted from the machines, 'Is that him?' 'Is that the one?' The group of men carrying me shouted back, 'Yes, yes, it's him, we've caught him at last!' One man stopped his machine and ran towards us, shouting, 'Wait, wait for me. I've been waiting for this for twelve years. Is that him?' 'Yes, it's him. Come along with us.'

The man joined on at the back. As the group bore me down the gangway, shouting and laughing, others joined them too, until soon everyone was stopping his machine as we passed and running to catch up.

Past rows of lathes they carried me, past little green offices from which white-faced people peered or emerged excitedly to join on. I wondered what could be going to happen to me.

A man in front seemed to have found some sort of megaphone, an old tin funnel I think it was, and he was shouting, 'Hear the news, hear this, brothers! See him, here he is! Come and see justice done, justice at last,' while the others seemed to be chanting the nine times multiplication table. A tall man in a trilby came striding along the edge of the group behind me, pushing people aside until he drew level. He reached up and grasped my shoulders, then pulled me down and thrust his face into mine. 'If my brother was working today,' he hissed, 'he'd be here too, you can take it from me.' He thrust me up again and disappeared into the crowd. Several people shouted, 'Yes, that's right!' and shook their fists at me. One man spat at me, but it didn't reach. Then a great cheer went up from everyone as a man stepped out into the path of the crowd unrolling a sort of banner. He handed one of its supports, which was an old broom with a broken head, to someone on the right of the man with the funnel, while he held up the other and walked on the left. The banner, whose message I could not see, stretched across in front of me like a sail, and I couldn't see ahead.

After a while I thought that it would be a good idea if I were to make some kind of protest. I decided that the best plan would be to try to explain everything as calmly and as quietly as I could to the nearest person, but I had only just begun to work out the best beginning when we suddenly stopped.

The banner came down, the chanting stopped. There was only the sound of coughing and a continuous noise of air rushing through something at a great rate. In front of me I could see rows of curtained sections stretching away into the distance. Then suddenly the curtains twitched and jerked, everywhere at once, and were all pulled back to reveal dozens of figures.

The most striking thing about them was their colour. Each man was covered entirely in a colour. Many of them were bright red, but each one a different shade of bright red and some were fluorescent almost. There were blues and yellows too, but dark greens predominated. They all wore goggles of one kind or another, and each one had his mouth and nose covered by a shaped and perforated mask from which peeped wisps of cotton wool or something. They all stood motionless looking at us. No one moved. Then one of the figures, a great red one, moved out of his bay and walked towards us, trailing behind him a pipe attached to a complicated gun-like instrument which he held in his hand. He came slowly up to me and stared. Several people coughed awkwardly.

Then he raised his goggles, took off his mask and burst into laughter. All the other figures did the same, and everyone in the procession started to laugh too. The place was full of the noise of laughter, and some of the men in the spray booths – for that, I realised, is what they were – were bent double or staggered about, while others ran towards us laughing and cheering. The procession started forward again with a jerk, almost overbalancing me. Up swung the banner in front of me, and the laughter gave way to 'Onward Christian Soldiers', which was taken up quickly and enthusiastically from those who had begun it. Everyone started to march in time then, and the procession speeded up a little. The spray-men had all joined the crowd and dotted it with bright colours.

The hymn swelled to a mighty chorus, and I saw that many people in the crowd held up rude banners or placards of one kind or another; but they were all so crudely made and hastily written that I couldn't read any of them, although I turned round as far as I could and tried very hard.

Now people were skipping and dancing all along both edges of the column, which had grown so long that I couldn't see the end of it. I saw a man running to overtake the crowd carrying a red coat or cloth or something. He reached the front of the column gasping for breath, raised the cloth and threw it up over me. My head came through a large tear in the middle of it so that it settled over my shoulders and dropped around me like a cloak, and the crowd cheered wildly at this. The cloth was very dirty, and smelt of cats. Then I saw behind me something like a long yellow top hat being passed over the heads of the crowd towards me, and presently it was set on my head by a tall man. Coloured streamers hung from the top of it and waved and fluttered about with the movement of those beneath me. Now a man was pushing a barrel-organ just in front of us, on which sat another man twirling a wooden rattle as hard as he could. The noise was deafening. I had to do something, something dramatic or violent to stop the procession at least. Then I could try to talk to someone and explain that this was all a dreadful mistake and that the real culprit had got away. I decided that I must kick one of the men carrying me in the chest with my heel, however unmannered such an action would be. If he staggered, or fell and dropped me, even, it would hold up the procession. Then I could shout out that I was innocent, and someone would have to listen to me.

I was about to raise my right foot when I was completely put off my balance by my bearers descending a step, one of them slightly before the other. I waved my arms in the air and regained balance, but immediately the same thing happened again, and I found that the whole procession was descending a stairway leading down into the ground. The men who were carrying me grunted and strained as they descended each step, and jolted me around a good deal so that I was unable to carry out my plan. I would wait until we reached the bottom. I waited some time, but the steps continued and my bearers staggered about more and more so that I thought they might very well trip and fall without my assistance. I twisted round as far as I could to see behind me. It was becoming dark. I saw the whole procession above me, rolling down the steps. The light shone briefly on the figures which were coming over the top, red men, black men, men in long leather aprons with shirtsleeves rolled up, then some bright blue men carrying placards; but as they descended into the gloom they all became just more or less grey figures, jostling, struggling, grunting, staggering drunkenly down step after step. I tried to look ahead down the stairs, but although the front banner now drooped disconsolately as its bearers concentrated on the stairs, the tunnel was so dark that I couldn't see anything but a few steps.

Most of the noise had subsided now. The band had stopped playing and the singing and cheering had given way first to humming and then to grunting and laboured breathing. Every so often someone would swear or groan, and everyone was too busy concentrating on the steps to talk to anyone else. The only loud noise was a rhythmic jangling crashing noise ahead of us, which I took to be the barrel-organ descending the stairs. Soon, I thought, that noise would stop, and we should be at the bottom of the stairs. But it went on and on, sometimes changing in tone as different parts of the organ were jarred. Then it alternated with a scraping noise, and I guessed that the rear wheels had both come off.

It was almost completely dark now, and while one of the men who was carrying me seemed fairly happy to step out into thin air each time, the other was nervous and insisted on feeling his way down each step with his foot. This threw us all off balance, which made the man even more nervous so that he tried to reach down with his free hand to feel the way, which was of course impossible and made the other man trip and almost overbalance. He shouted a curse at his partner, who gasped that he would have to rest. The confident man said that he could do with one too, but that the bottom of the stairway was probably only a few steps away and they should carry on. The first man said yes, of course, it couldn't be far away, and we staggered on. After a while the nervous man, who was finding the going very difficult, said that he couldn't go any further even if the very next step was the last one, but the other man made him go two more steps to find out. It wasn't the bottom, so the confident man said well, just once more, but the other said no, and stopped. But the people immediately behind us were so engrossed in going down the steps that either they wouldn't stop, or when they realised that we had stopped were pushed on by the people behind them. It was completely dark now. The man who wanted to rest shouted out angrily that someone was stepping on his foot, and someone behind shouted back that they had to carry on even if they did step on our feet because the people behind them wouldn't stop. So the other man who was carrying me let out a great bellow that everyone must stop, but it was drowned by an outcry of people just behind us complaining that the people behind them were stepping on their feet, and the reply from further back that it couldn't be helped because all the people further back were pushing. All this was in pitch darkness.

At length all the shouting and pushing subsided, and the two men put me down slowly and with much grunting. I groped downwards but could feel nothing but damp steps as far as my hand would reach. A man shouted, 'Let's deal with him now.' This was received by a tired cheer, which echoed and reverberated around for several seconds. We were certainly not at the bottom of the steps, and when another voice, further away, shouted, 'What shall we do with him, then?' the answer was so obvious that I immediately shouted as loudly as I possibly could, 'I am innocent!'

When the echoes of my voice had died away there was complete silence, so I seized the opportunity of shouting it again, and added, 'And I've just about had enough of all this nonsense!' An uncouth voice yelled from the darkness 'We want justice!' and with that there was a roar of cheering and clapping and whistling which shook the steps and echoed up and down like the waves of the sea. Immediately it subsided I countered, 'This is England in the twentieth century and if you want justice I demand a trial by jury.' That would shake them, I had thought – but there was instantly such a howling and roaring of laughter that I thought the roof would cave in, and the air rang and reverberated as if we were inside a great bell. As it quietened again the same rough voice shouted back, 'Well, there's 'undreds of us, mate, and we're all unanimous.' I replied, 'This is a democracy and a free country, and a man shall be tried by his peers!' A thinner, slightly more cultured voice with a sort of lisp called back, 'What? Shall we fill all the jury boxes with perverts? A man shall be tried by decent respectable citizens, which is a fair description of everyone here excluding you.' 'But this is mob rule,' I protested, 'we live in a democracy, not a dictatorship.' The cultured voice told me to make up my mind whether I was objecting to mob rule or to dictatorship. 'I am not in a mood for argument,' I shouted, 'I demand my rights!' I would have banged once or twice on a table at that point, or made some fierce gesture, but neither was possible. 'Wights?' lisped a voice. 'What are these wights?' 'Rights!' I said, 'Sacred, inalienable and incontrovertible!' 'Piffle,' said the voice. 'We're ordinary men, we don't hold with airy-fairy ideas. You have no wights, only neighbours. Only us and our inclinations. Your wights are whatever we happen to be feeling like, and don't forget it.' 'I never heard such nonsense!' I shouted. 'Of course there are rights.' 'Where?' said the voice, jeering. 'In books?' 'They lie,' I said, 'at the very roots of our society.' 'Exactly,' it answered, 'and we are that society, all of us here together. We have decided to give you the wight to be punished. When you have been helped by us to use this wight then justice will have been done.' 'But I am innocent,' I protested. 'How can all this be justice if I am innocent?' 'Justice,' lisped the voice, 'is not a matter of innocence or guilt. Justice is not concerned with truth at all, but with evidence. If all the men in all the prisons of England were found to have been wrongly convicted and all the men who ever hung from a British gallows-post innocent, it would cast no shadow on our justice, because justice has nothing to do with clairvoyance. If you are innocent that is your own affair, our proper concern is the evidence.'

At this a great cheer went up and I felt a solid wall of hands pushing at me from the steps above. I went down a few of the steps, but they followed me down and pushed me again. In the darkness it felt as if the whole tunnel was blocked by a barrier of hands, which moved slowly down the tunnel like a plunger. I collided with the barrel organ on my way down. After twenty or so quick steps I stopped to think what I should do, but before many seconds had passed a cold palm touched my cheek, and the hands pushed me silently off the step. I ran down a few more steps and stopped again, but the hands caught up with me this time before I could sit down, and I was forced to keep moving continuously down. This was a desperate situation, and called for desperate measures. I put my hand in my pocket and pulled out my pocket-knife. It was small but sharp, but in order to open it I had to use both hands. So it was that when the hands next bumped into me I overbalanced and fell, and started to slide and roll down the steps quite helplessly and very fast.

chapter six

When one is suddenly placed in a situation of extreme danger, so that one looks, so to speak, into the mouth of death, the mind transcends fear and panic and achieves in the instant a steel cold calm which resists both pain and mutilation and lasts, so I have been told, as long as consciousness itself. As I tumbled, bumping and rolling down through the darkness, I remember that, although I was quite convinced that I should soon be dead, I had reasoned that I might as well try to take the blows as strategically as possible. Even somersaulting over and over I had presence of mind and orientation enough to be able to bring my right shoulder round to take a large proportion of the collisions, and I remember trying to recall the anatomical diagrams I had studied as a schoolboy, in order to assess the relative damage which various parts of my body could take before I should be forced to manoeuvre another part round to the front. I was beginning to think that my right shoulder had had enough, and that it would be interesting to see how they set a collar bone, when I landed at the bottom of the stairs.

I landed my proper way up and as softly as if in a pile of feathers, but the smell was revolting. I was sitting up to my armpits in a thick, lumpy liquid which was slightly fluorescent, and couldn't possibly be anything else but sewage. Oh, blessed sewage. I felt my shoulder. I was bruised but, I thought, nothing more. I looked over the slight fluorescence which was all round me and decided that I must be in a large cellar or cesspit of some kind. I did not favour trying to climb the stairs again. I saw a slight glow or light of some kind across the way, and decided to wade through the sludge to find out what it was. The liquid was up to my waist, but as I was thoroughly soaked in the filth already this didn't bother me.

The light was further away and brighter than I thought, for I waded across this sea of filth for a quarter of an hour or so before I became certain that it was in fact a lamp of some kind. It was difficult to see clearly because steamy mists puffed about on the surface of the ooze like ghosts. Five minutes later I made out a figure sitting beneath the light, and five minutes after that I was within hailing distance.

As I waded towards the figure it jumped up and faced me as if alarmed, and I realised that although my top-hat had gone I still had the red cloak on and the trimmings hung round me, and I might look rather strange. I took these off and threw them aside as I waded. Now I could see that the man was in a rowing-boat, with the lamp on the top of its mast. Eventually he decided that I was human, and punted the boat over towards me.

He stopped a little way away from me and barked, 'Who are you, then?' and began to punt round and round me, about ten feet away. 'Me?' I said. 'Smallcreep, Pinquean Smallcreep, works number 1644/254.' 'What department is that?' he demanded. 'Slotters,' I said. He stopped the boat and let go of the pole, which stood upright in the ooze, and took a little book from his pocket. 'Oh yes,' he said, thumbing through it. 'Slotters is above grinders and above turners.' 'Is that so?' I said. 'Yes, and above shapers and drillers and above fettlers and sanders.' 'Really,' I said. He went on, 'But not above millers or routers, and not above setters or fitters or dressers or viewers.' He snapped the book shut. 'Just as long as I know,' he said, and took the pole in both hands and pushed his way over to me. 'Climb in,' he ordered. I did so, and he turned the boat and poled slowly along as if through treacle.

The smell of the place had begun to impress itself on me. Earlier on, any smell had been the sweet smell of life, but now I realised that the air here was quite definitely the foulest I had ever breathed, and I almost retched. It was so foul that it tasted sweet in my mouth and stung my eyes, and sweat broke out all over my face and neck. My companion, who wore thigh-boots and a sou'wester, with a red velvet jacket in between, told me that his name was Walpole and that his works number was number one. 'Not because I was the first person to be employed in this factory,' he explained. 'That would be impossible, of course. It is because' – and here he stopped punting and took off his sou'wester – 'because I am the lowest, in every sense of the word.' 'In every sense?' I asked. 'In every sense,' he said. 'This is the lowest level of the factory, mine is the humblest job, and I am paid the lowest wage in the whole establishment.' 'How dreadful for you,' I said. 'I beg your pardon,' he said, sounding hurt. 'I am extremely proud and extremely lucky to have such a place. My wife patches and mends and improvises heroically and we gladly and proudly go without practically everything.'

He replaced his hat and began poling the boat again. Bubbles of gas blurted up wherever he put down the pole, and left little fluorescent patches in the air behind us. 'Surely,' I said, 'it would be possible for you to secure a better wage. Won't your Union back you up?' At this, he looked so offended that I hastily added '– or don't you see eye to eye with the Unions?', but then he looked even more indignant and said I ought to know that I was speaking to a lifelong and fully paid-up member of the Confederated Society of Gutsmen and Trodge-sluggers, who would like to meet any working-class man who could be so cowardly and treacherous as to raise objections, however conscientious, to joining his appointed Union, who could so desecrate the graves of his forefathers, who could spit into the torch which had been brought so far at such great cost, who could snub so long-standing and respectable a working-class institution. 'We must all stand firm behind the Labour Movement,' he said. 'It is our sacred duty.' 'I am with you there, brother,' I said. 'Then surely the Union would help you to better your position here –' 'I should certainly hope not,' he replied. 'Are you telling me to ask them to upset the entire system of wage differential upon which the Unions, and indeed all society stand? Unions exist to create and preserve order and syntax in our society, not to back up the haphazard fancies of greedy and irresponsible minorities or individuals.' I said that I thought he might have secured a few shillings more a week without serious consequences, but he replied that he was, only just below, for instance, sweepers and scrubbers. 'And you know what they're like,' he said. 'My wife wouldn't like to think that I was doing the same class of work as people who get down on their hands and knees to scrub floors. She'd say to me, "Walpole", she'd say, "what's the damned use of you bringing me home all this money to buy food and things with if we're going to be on a level with that sort of person? What's the use of money to buy new clothes with if you can't hold up your head in the street?" she'd say. And it wouldn't be long before all the sweepers and scrubbers and sealers and trimmers and dustmen and mortuary cleaners and all the rest of the rabble would up and shout "Walpole down in the pit has secured a rise, we must re-establish the differential", and so they would, and then it would be the drain-cleaners and second-class incinerator chargers and tip attendants who'd start, and so on, and, well, you heard what the Prime Minister said only last week.'

I still thought it very unfair, and began to make another suggestion, but he cut in, 'Oh, it isn't as if we don't *need* the money. We've four enormous children, and an invalid mother with us, and I'd like to be able to take a day or two off sometimes when there's not so much work here, because the wife has funny turns when things get too much for her, and sometimes I have to dig up one of the children or fish the baby out of the waterbutt and revive it after I come home from work. It's very wearing on all of us, and a bit more money *would* make a difference. But that isn't the point, we know quite well we don't deserve it.'

The end of his pole bounced off something floating just beneath the surface of the liquid, making a noise like a muffled drum. 'What's that?' I asked, but then I saw by the light of the lamp a circle of dark hair floating on the surface, spreading out and drawing in, with a whitish patch peeping from the centre of it. It looked like some disgusting jellyfish-animal which might have been created spontaneously in such a coacervation of filth. 'A floater,' he said. 'There are several down here, they come and go, and move about as if they were able to swim.' He pushed the thing away, and it gave a rolling heave like a dead whale before disappearing into the darkness and mist.

He continued to pole. We seemed to be going from nowhere into nowhere, with only the lumpy texture of the surface of the ooze to indicate that we were moving at all. 'No,' he went on, 'we can't really claim to deserve it. I never gave up any time to study when I was young. When other young chaps were hard at work every evening all alone studying mathematics or electronics, I was wasting my time talking to people, or writing poetry, or trying to play the trumpet or something. You'd never believe it, I used to just talk to people for hours and hours, about nothing in particular. When my friends were spending their money on encyclopaedias and slide rules, I was wasting mine on fishing rods and photography and so on, or just putting it away in the bank. I met the wife when we were both fifteen, and we used to spend most of the time just enjoying ourselves together, you know, going about to films and concerts, and reading together, or just talking to people. So you see we really don't deserve any of the luxuries which other people made sacrifices for. Some of them hated every minute of it, some of them had their fathers standing over them with stock whips, or had their pocket money stopped every time they slacked. Most of them hate the jobs they do now and come out in rashes and spots and get ulcers, or shout at their children and go to bed. Now me, I almost like my job sometimes, down here on my own, no one to bother me. So how could I possibly expect much wages?'

But I wasn't satisfied. 'Surely yours is a very responsible job, then?' I said. 'I couldn't really say that,' he replied. 'Up there everyone depends on everyone else. If the lower miller makes a mistake the whole line gets jammed up, and if a foreman or, say, a chief fitter makes a mistake or falls ill whole sections of the factory become unworkable in a few days. How could I, a mere remover of sewage compare myself with people like that? And it's not only that: when they pay us lower people a lot of money it's because we've been unreasonable and selfish and refuse to do the job, but when they pay them big salaries up there it's because they have to, to get the right man.' I said that I had to admit the weight of these arguments and that perhaps, after all, he was right to accept his present position in all humility. 'You are a man of fibre,' I said. 'But for men like you our country would not be what it is, I am certain.' He looked embarrassed, and muttered something about honour and duty.

There was a little light coming from above us now, as if through frosted glass. I could see no walls around us, or any horizon to the sea of sewage, but ahead of us there seemed to be a kind of island, very small, not even big enough to build the smallest house on, but very solid, with square edges as if it was made of concrete. On it stood a tower of steel latticework which soared out of sight into the darkness and mist above us. As we came closer I saw that the island was in fact a concrete platform, and the tower on it had a sliding telescopic door in it which made me realise that the tower was the bottom of a lift shaft. After another five minutes of strong poling we tied up to the island and stepped on to it.

'I'll get you a change of clothes and then we'll send you up in the lift,' he said. 'I'll call him now,' and he pressed a button on the corner of the tower before shuffling round to the other side, squeaking his thighboots together. In a few seconds he reappeared carrying a complete set of clothes, brand new overall and all. 'Change,' he said. 'But I can't take these from you,' I protested. 'It's O.K., I'll keep yours, you see. I have my own stuff washed regularly, one more change won't make any difference.' I accepted them and thanked him, and started to change quickly, for the lift had been called. Seeing my haste he laughed and said that if I was hurrying for the lift I shouldn't bother, because it would probably be a very long time. 'He spends most of his time at the top.' 'The top?' I said. 'Yes, this lift goes all the way through the departments to the very top, the managing director. He's the one end, I'm at the other. Makes me kind of proud. If I didn't smell so bad I'd go right up one day and shake him by the hand, though it would take me all day to get there and back.'

He was busying himself opening little iron trapdoors which were in rows all along the edge of the island. Having opened them all, he began to go from one to the other, peering closely into them. 'They tell me that up there,' he went on, speaking as he worked, 'right at the top, is a place where they do nothing but shovel money about, just as I shovel shit.' 'Surely not,' I said. 'That's what they say, and Ovine, that's the man who runs the lift, says that up there you turn on the taps and whisky comes out and everything's solid gold, the chairs, tables, doors, everything, and the carpets are mink. Just fancy treading on mink.' 'I don't believe it,' I said. He shrugged, and, having peered down the last hole, skiff-skiffed off in his thigh boots round to the other side of the lift-shaft.

I had finished changing now, and looked up the shaft as far as I could see, but no sign of the lift. I thought that if it didn't come soon my clothes would be as smelly as they were before I changed. Walpole returned with a long rod of metal which had a T-handle on one end and a socket on the other. He lifted another trapdoor and plunged the rod down into it. 'Well, I don't know what to believe,' he said feeling around with the rod. 'It's not for the likes of you and me to bother our heads about anyway.' He found whatever it was he was feeling for, turned the handle a little to the right and scuttled over to the little trapdoors to continue peering into them. I heard a sort of gurgling noise coming from some of them and a loud hissing came from others, all to the evident satisfaction of my friend, who began to shuttle between the handle and the holes with the concentration of an engine driver. He continued in this way for what seemed a very long time, sometimes whistling through his teeth busily to himself, sometimes seeming to count quietly to himself. We said nothing to each other for what seemed hours, and I could only stand with my hands in my pockets and watch him, or watch the fantastic shapes of the drifting mists which moved silently and slowly around us.

Suddenly there was a loud noise high above us in the tower, which sounded like a stone rattling down the inside of a drainpipe. Walpole did not pause or lift his head, but pointed upwards and said 'Ovine'. Ovine it was, and coming so fast I thought that he must have had some accident and be in free fall. The lift came to a halt with a crash and a twanging and rattling of cables. I stepped up to the doors and looked through the latticework into the lift, but could see no one inside. There was no light in there. I turned towards my friend, but he was counting and taking no notice of me, so I grasped the brass handle of the door and drew it across. There was a dreadful squeaking of un-lubricated metal. Then I opened the door of the lift itself, which was better lubricated, and stepped inside.

Of Ovine there was no sign, and inside the lift it was almost dark. On the opposite wall was a large panel covered with a vast number of labelled buttons, and in the corner stood an upright coffin complete with lid. The two doors closed behind me, but the lift did not move. I was a little impatient by now, so that when I heard a muttering noise coming from the coffin I approached it and knocked smartly on its lid. The muttering continued, so I put my ear to the lid. Someone seemed to be addressing someone else on the subject of rabbit-breeding inside there, but how two people could have got inside I could not imagine. 'Be careful of a diet over-rich in cabbage or dandelions in the first few weeks, or they get scours and blow up like balloons and die in agony,' said the voice. I rapped on the lid again and the voice said, 'Goodness me, someone at the door, please excuse me.' The lid fell down on the floor with a crash, revealing the back of a man wearing a long black belted overcoat and Wellington boots. He seemed to have been smoking a pipe in there, for foul tobacco smoke filled the coffin. He stepped out as smartly as if he normally walked backwards, and smiled at me. 'Ovine Fudge,' he said. 'Pleased to meet you.' 'How do you do? Pinquean Smallcreep,' I said. 'Charmed. By the way, I hope you didn't think that I was talking to myself in there,' he said. I politely replied that of course I didn't, and would he be so good as to take me up to the Assembly Line. 'Yes, lots of people hear me talking away like that and think I'm mad or something, but actually I'm not talking to myself at all, I'm talking to the lift.' 'It just shows you,' I said, 'Just as I always say, everything has a rational explanation.' He went on, 'It's the same with all machinery, now, the pieceworkers say the same.' 'Oh yes,' I said, interested. 'Yes, at one time man was master of the machine and made it do his bidding without question. All that's finished now.'

He was a small man with small features, a small chin, a small mouth with a small moustache underneath a small nose. Two little piggy eyes close together, a short brow and a small area of well groomed hair. Only his ears were large, and long hairs stuck out of them like rabbit's whiskers. He smoked a small foul smelling pipe. He went on, 'It's not as if the machines have become the masters or anything like that. It's much more subtle, it's somehow as if the machines have joined themselves on to us through long intercourse, so that you sometimes aren't sure if it's you moving the machine or the machine moving you to move it. If you come to work in the morning in a bad mood, you find the machine behaving badly too. All the time it reflects you. They all do it, not only lifts.' I said that I had heard this feeling expressed by other machine operators too. 'So I make things easier by recognising them as equals straight away, and trying a bit of give and take sometimes. This lift and I get along fine, and he's a great talker.' 'And a great listener,' I said. 'He certainly is,' he replied.

I asked him if it would be possible to go up soon, if only to get some fresh air as soon as possible. 'I'll ask him nicely,' he said, 'but you have to be careful. You see, it goes far deeper than just polite conversation. They can read your very thoughts. I don't like it at all, day in, day out. I feel like a skinned rabbit some days.' I said that it was always good to get away from the machines at the end of the day. 'It certainly is,' he said sadly, 'and that's what worries me so much. People step into my lift all day saying "Roll on half-past five," and I say "Yes, roll on half-past five," and then about Wednesday we start saying "Roll on the weekend," and ten to one by Saturday teatime, what with one thing and another, I'll be saying to myself, "Roll on Monday morning, when I can start work again." But then, just after Christmas everyone who uses the lift says "Roll on the summer holidays!" and just after we come back from them everyone starts saying "Roll on Christmas", but we all know damn well that we'll be bored stiff half-way through the holidays and sick and tired of Christmas before it's Boxing Day, and then all you've got to look forward to is coming back to work again. So then anyone over the age of thirty I meet will be saying "Roll on when we retire", and of course I agree with them. But we all know very well that after a year or so of retirement we shall be sick to death of it.' He paused to stuff his pipe, which had gone out, with a fresh charge of an evil looking black flake tobacco which he seemed to keep loose in one of the pockets of his overcoat. He lit the pipe again carefully, caressing it with three matches in succession, sucking loudly and vigorously and puffing out great clouds of smoke at me.

'So I've come to terms with that too, as you can see,' he nodded towards the coffin. 'Ovine, I said to myself one day, let's have no more of this self-deception. Make up your mind where you're going, I said, and act accordingly. So I bought three of these – one for work, one for relaxation and one to sleep in.' He stroked the coffin affectionately. 'Nice piece of wood,' he said. 'Cost a penny too. Nothing elaborate, mind – simple and good. My wife's got a nice pair too. Whenever we feel a bit off-colour we run and get into them. The wife had all our children in her bedroom one. We lie side by side in them at nights and talk about the notices we'll get in the papers. It's wonderful, we make up a new one for each other every night, so that if in the morning one of us has passed away, the other will have it fresh in mind. She's done some lovely ones for me. "Fudge, Ovine. God took your hand, we had to part, He eased your pain but broke my heart." There, isn't that nice? That's if I die of anything painful. Then there's "Words cannot express this tragic loss, lovingly remembered and never forgotten." It's very difficult to find anything to rhyme with forgotten. Only rotten and only-begotten, and they're not much use. I could go on for hours, "Fudge, Emily. Will be sadly missed along life's way, but regularly remembered every day. Safe in the arms of Jesus." Then there'll be the little bits from our children. "Fudge, Ovine and Emily. Reunited. Loving memories of dear Mum and Dad. They gave us years of happiness with their kind and loving ways, then left us beautiful memories, to treasure the rest of our days. Ethel, Belinda and Harry." "Treasured memories, never to forget, always remembered, forever in our thoughts. Loving thoughts and kind memories in our hearts forever. Ada, Ethel, Thelma, Roy, daughters, Freddie and Harold, granddaughters, sons-in-law, nephews and Auntie Doris and Tom." Isn't that lovely? They made those up. Then there'd be the acknowledgements. "The relatives of Ovine and Emily Fudge wish to thank all friends and neighbours and members of the House of Faith and the Bedminster Corps Salvationists for their kindly thoughts and flowers and wreaths and prayers and letters of sympathy and memories at the time of their recent sad loss."'

I said how wonderful to have a family and relatives who thought so much of you, but he said that actually they all hated each other and didn't get on at all well. 'Family reunion parties are nightmares,' he said. 'Only this death business brings us together at all, that's half the wonder of it.' He dreamed to himself for a second, then said, 'I often wonder what it will be – cancer, stroke, pneumonia – I had a cough the other day – or suicide even.' 'Oh no!' I said, genuinely shocked, 'That's just cowardly talk.' 'Cowardly? I reckon it's pretty marvellous myself. Heroic, when you come to think of it.' 'Nonsense,' I said. 'Well, they have memorials all over the place to people who gave their lives in battle, and they'd have avoided it if they could. The suicide doesn't ask favours of anyone else, or make a fuss. He dies by his own hand and his own will. 'Good heavens, if killing yourself didn't take more courage than most of us have, none of us would survive more than twenty years.' 'It's most immoral,' I said. 'Well, if you ask me, the moral position of a man who commits suicide is pretty sound. We only ask a man to give his life as a punishment for the most serious crimes of all. How can we possibly blame a suicide for anything less?'

I found the discussion very distasteful, but he would not stop. 'Now, just imagine yourself in the place of a man about to take his own life. How stupid and trivial all the worries and grumbles of everyone else must seem, and you wouldn't be worried by debts any more, or pain, or wanting the woman next door. All the policemen and nagging wives and screaming children and the blasted foreman, poof! all gone in a second. What was it someone said now – yes – "... the noblest of men; and other men, loathe to concede their own cowardice, defile his grave with epitaphs questioning the balance of his mind, and close the stable door with laws." Heroic that's what I call it.' He stood for some while in quiet contemplation, his head on one side, an expression of sad bliss on his face.

After a time I cleared my throat and remarked that I thought we ought to be getting up now. He jumped up out of his trance and said to no one in particular, 'Well, then, how do you feel about it, shall we be going up now? I think you've had long enough rest, you know.' He went over to the panel and pressed several buttons at once. For a second or two nothing happened, so that I was about to say that the lift seemed to favour resting a little longer. Then it was as if I was hit on the soles of my feet by a sledgehammer, and my stomach was being dragged out of the bottom of me, and my head pressed down into my shoulders. The lift was banging about in the shaft now, and my feet seemed to be moving about all over the place under me while my body stayed still. My ears felt as if they would burst inside my head, and then they did, with a pop, and I felt much better.

Ovine had shown no signs of any discomfort, and was now looking furtively around him as if he suspected that there might be someone else hiding in the lift, which was ridiculous. Then he sidled up to me and drew from inside his coat a small red plastic object about the size of a small box of chocolates. 'Look,' he said, 'what I bought yesterday.' 'That's rather smart,' I said. 'What is it?' 'It's wonderful,' he went on, 'you can do anything with it. It's guaranteed absolutely shockproof.' 'Really,' I said. 'Yes, and completely self-winding and self-regulating. Listen!' He held it to my ear. It was making a quiet humming noise. 'You see? And look, it's got a row of funny faces all round it just like in the newspapers.' I looked and it had. 'What's that?' I asked, and pointed to a little glass tube which was let into one corner, like a spirit level. He giggled. 'Oh that. Well, it's that, look.' He tipped the whole thing ninety degrees and a tiny effigy of a woman in frilly underclothes slid down the tube. 'See – it's marvellous, isn't it?' He was smiling now, and searched my face for approval or wonder. 'You see? You see?' 'Amazing,' I admitted, and secretly thought that all this joy was indeed amazing in one so preoccupied with death only a few moments ago. This must be a wonderful device. 'What exactly is it for?' I asked. 'Well, look,' he said, 'it's got what they call a magic eye.' I said I'd heard of such things, but knew nothing about them. 'Well, look, you see there it is, in that little window there. See? It shines out at you, look, and it tells you how bright it is, according to the temperature and so on. Just at a glance. Press this button here, look, and out it goes. On again look – then out!' He burst out in a little shout of delight, then went on, 'Look, and here there's three little bubbles floating in green oil that show you how far on it is, and a dial that goes up to forty thousand radiations.' 'Amazing,' I said. 'That's not all of it,' he went on excitedly. 'This part here opens up and you can keep things in it, things, anything you want to. Lots of handy partitions, you could do anything you wanted. And a quick release catch, see, snap! just like that, handy if you're in a hurry, see.'

The lift was carrying us upwards very fast, and I wondered if we might overshoot wherever it was I wanted to go, but then I thought that it was all probably automatic, and that there was no need to worry. He went on, 'The cigar-trimmer part doesn't seem to work, but I don't smoke cigars so that doesn't matter. Isn't it smart? All smooth, and a lovely colour. You feel, look, you feel and stroke it. Lovely finish.' I took it carefully in both hands. It was very heavy. 'Go on,' he said impatiently. 'Go on, stroke it.' I stroked it then he grabbed it back again and stuffed it into his coat. 'Just having it in my coat makes me feel bright and streamlined and modern.' 'I'm sure it does,' I said. 'I saw it on television, Smarty Wiseman was using it at a party. Smarty Wiseman himself!' I said I didn't care for Smarty Wiseman much. 'Too cheeky,' I said. 'Yes, but he's clever, you must admit he's clever.' He glanced at me suspiciously. 'You're the first person I've met who doesn't like Smarty Wiseman,' he said with disapproval. 'I – I'm sorry,' I said nervously. 'Well, anyway, some engine-drivers were using one too, in a pub. On the telly, of course,' he added quickly, as if he thought I didn't believe him.

He looked quickly at an indicator above the door, turned to the panel and pressed some buttons. We decelerated, which was like falling and made me feel sick briefly. We clattered to a halt, then jumped upwards twice and downwards once. Wild faces peered through the doors, which were then torn open to admit a crowd of fierce men, all growling and muttering. For a moment I thought that they intended to attack us, but instead they milled round and round in the none-too-large lift like penned bulls, buffeting Ovine and myself about. One of them slammed the doors shut and motioned fiercely to Ovine that they wished to go up. After a few seconds we moved up, more gently this time and without swaying about. I glanced at Ovine, and saw that he was now dressed in a grey jacket with a badge on the pocket and silver buttons. The men all wore thick leather aprons like slices of bread. All had several days' stubble on their chins, and glared about and crunched their teeth together. Some had their arms folded, others clenched and unclenched their fists and none of them seemed capable of standing still. The lift was packed with us all, but they jostled and squeezed around, muttering to each other and spitting on the floor. Then one of them, who wore a red silk scarf round his neck like a cowboy, said in a loud voice, 'Brothers,' and all the others said, 'Aye!' and turned round to face him. He went on, 'We stand together here, and we shall stand firm together!' 'Aye!' said the rest. 'And standing firm together, we shall stand together to fight on the struggle together!' 'Aye!' in unison. 'And standing thus firm together –' 'Aye!' 'we shall not fall, but shall rise up and fall on our chains!' 'Aye!' 'Shoulder to shoulder we shall hold fast, and in the face of every determination, we shall stand forth everything that comes before us!'

The rest of the men gave a great cheer, and the man who was addressing them pushed the coffin over with a crash and stepped up on to it. 'Brothers! United in this one accord we shall mount the barricades and sweep away all barriers! In your humility realise your excellence! In your impartiality tolerate nothing which you believe to be false! In your meekness do not shrink from total power!' All the other fierce men shouted 'Hoorah!' at this, and stamped their hobnailed boots on the metal floor until I thought we should all go through it. But the one who was speaking held up his hand for silence.

'The time has come, my brothers, to strive and strain to bring about what cannot be prevented! And so I say, brothers, Rise up! Rise up!' At this they all went absolutely wild, and growled and snarled and kicked the walls of the lift, and jumped and stamped and shouted and held up their hands as if they were strangling somebody. Ovine, who now seemed to be dressed in a splendid red overcoat with gold epaulettes and braid and gold buttons down the back, with white gloves over his left shoulder, was pushing buttons frantically. We decelerated alarmingly so that for a second we all left the floor, and the men raged around weightlessly in all directions and all ways up. So it was that when the doors opened and they tumbled out in a sort of struggling heap, I was carried out too and swept along by the storm of their eagerness, until it was too late for me to turn back because the lift doors had closed. I had no idea where I was, but these men seemed to have every idea and so I allowed myself to be carried along by them, in fact, I hardly had any alternative if I wished not to be trampled on by at least half the hobnailed boots.

As we rushed along I could see that we were on the office floor, which is one floor above the factory shop-floor. I had never been here before, but I could hear the muffled roar of the machinery below us. We were travelling along a corridor which was not straight but turned at right-angles to the left or right at intervals of a few yards and made the going at that speed very difficult. The group seemed to negotiate these corners mainly by crashing into the opposite wall and rebounding, which I found very wearing. Then we slowed down a little and the men began pulling their clothes about and dusting their trousers and trying to rub the toe of one boot on the back of the opposite trouser leg, which is of course impossible while walking so that they all tripped each other up and swore at each other and the red handkerchief man put his finger up to his mouth and shushed as loud as a steam-engine. They were walking more slowly now, and seemed to crouch a little, like men approaching a dangerous animal. A door faced us ahead, which had written on it in black letters 'Neg. Off.' Everyone decreased speed so persistently then that I thought that by some mathematical law we should never actually reach the door. But we did, and then stood quietly round it, the men all looking at each other, as if each expected someone else to do something.

Now I must politely leave them, I thought; but before I could say a word the door had opened and a voice ordered us to come in. I had no intention of going in, but the others had suddenly become like sleepwalkers and moved in through the door in a column, carrying me with them. The room was completely empty of all furniture and quite large. In the far corner squatted a group of elderly men very smartly dressed in black suits, sitting with their knees drawn up and chatting and smoking together. All of our group sat down in the corner by the door, myself in the middle. If I walked out now, I thought, it would seem very rude, and I decided to stay quiet until a better opportunity for leaving presented itself.

Now there was silence, but before long everybody seemed to get restless and some of our group started whispering loudly at the one in the red handkerchief, while the men in the other corner nudged each other about and shot glances at us across the room. Finally one of them stood up and called something to us, but he spoke with such an incredibly educated accent that I couldn't make out a word. The men in my group became terribly agitated then, and nudged and fidgeted about and whispered and finally pushed red handkerchief up on his feet and held him there. He stood there half standing and half sitting, like a child wanting to go to the toilet, and muttered something unintelligible about wanting to go to the toilet. His mates all hissed 'Gooarn!' at him, and the man on the other side who was still standing said, 'Dwoo spick arp' in his dreadfully correct accent. Red handkerchief started then in a strangely high pitched voice, and went on at some length while the others nodded from time to time; but his voice was so ridiculously quiet that even

I couldn't hear what he was saying, and I was sure that the other group couldn't. When he finally finished all the other men round me said 'Hear, hear!' and 'Very well expressed', and one of them shouted across to the other group, 'There you are, you see?' but the others went 'shish' at him.

The men in suits fidgeted about uncomfortably for a while, clearing their throats and hitching up their socks, then their spokesman stood up again. He began to make a speech to us in his high educated voice all about frankness and something about a spirit of quiet and calm determination, and how they were all convinced that all human problems could be solved in a civilised manner by the use of reason. Then he said that they had every intention of listening to our point of view sympathetically and without bias, and ended with the words 'And would you thyarfore please spik arp, as we cennort hyar a ward', and sat down. The men in our group whispered to each other frantically then, and eventually pushed red handkerchief up again. He gave a second performance no more audible than the first, which they punctuated with 'Exactly', and 'That's it', and when he finished they all clapped briefly and looked across to the other group to see what the reaction might be. It was much the same as before, and after a while their spokesman got up and stood awkwardly with his legs crossed clearing his throat and twiddling his pencil, and didn't seem to know what to say to us. The others in his group muttered at him impatiently and then he thanked us while the others nodded to each other quickly. Then he said that with our permission he would like us to hear the management's point of view on the matter. Our group said yes, certainly, so he sat down and another man in a black suit stood up. He had a tiny moustache and a bald head, and held a fat file under one arm. His top pocket bulged with all manner of gold and silver pens. He gripped the lapels of his jacket with both hands, so that he looked as if he rather fancied himself standing up and speaking like this, and he sort of tilted his head back a little and closed his eyes and screwed his mouth up into a little round O before starting to speak.

He began, 'It appears too arse ...' but then his phrasing became so strange, and the words he used so difficult, and his sentences so long and the whole speech so rambling and complex, that I very soon had no idea what he was talking about, and judging by the looks which my companions exchanged between themselves, they had no idea either. When the man finally sat down amid the enthusiastic congratulations of his friends all the men in our group shuffled about on their bottoms and kicked each other and poked the red handkerchief man and made him stand up again. Again he protested that he wanted to go to the toilet, but they all hissed, 'Go on, go on,' so he cleared his throat and called across the room that it had certainly been a magnificent speech and no one could have put things more clearly, but he regretted that one or two of the points had gone over the heads of one or two of his group, and could they please possibly be so good as to repeat it all, 'in a slightly simpler way'.

The men in suits all frowned and muttered together, and then the first one stood up again. 'Ay shall repeat ar tarms in sentences of not mooer than fave wards,' he said, and began to do so, but his accent was so incredibly correct that it didn't sound like the English language at all, at least not what I'd call English, and I soon couldn't make out a word of it.

He went on for what seemed like half-an-hour, during which time two of our people fell asleep and started to snore, and had to be nudged violently. When he finally sat down his companions all gave little chuckles and patted him affectionately on the back, and smiled benevolently across at us. But when our spokesman was eventually persuaded to stand up and stammer out politely that we hadn't understood again, they all groaned and covered their eyes and ears with their hands and rocked backwards and forwards. Then there was an incredibly embarrassing silence during which I could hear somebody's wristwatch ticking and somebody else's stomach rumbling and red handkerchief whispering that he must go to the lavatory. Everybody in the room looked as if they would like the floor to give way and let them through. It was all nothing to do with me, of course, but I felt at least as embarrassed as everyone else.

Just as I felt that I couldn't bear it any longer and would have to ask someone the time just in order to hear a human voice again, there was a great flash of light in the centre of the room and suddenly there was a man spinning and somersaulting like a top in the air. He landed lightly and bowed to us both in turn. He was dressed in a smart set of blue overalls. 'Allow me to introduce myself, gentlemen. I am Brother Knarf, a professional industrial negotiator.' There was such an explosion of relief in the room that everyone, including myself, burst out laughing, or cheered, and some of us rose to shake hands with the opportune Brother Knarf. But he silenced and reseated us with a gesture of both arms, and then began to talk.

'There is some failure to communicate, some misunderstanding. Gentleman, may I offer you my services? Let me be your dragoman, your bridge, your ladder, your light, let me do your talking, let me talk your problems into extinction. I can talk your language, gentlemen, and yours. I have negotiated between Oxford dons and Irish whores, between a West End barrow boy and the Queen of Lithuania. I can speak with any accent in any dialect of any language spoken on the whole surface of the earth. I can speak in a high voice or a low voice. I can coo like a dove, roar like a lion or shout like thunder. I can imitate anybody I like; sometimes I talk like the Prime Minister, sometimes like the leader of the opposition. On occasions I make myself sound like a high-court judge, on others I whine and wheedle like the most wretched criminal. I have the whole range of human emotions at my fingertips like the keys of a piano, and with three words could get you all up on your feet dancing with joy and with three more instantly throw you all to the ground sobbing with grief. I can talk a corporation omnibus through the eye of a needle and all the beer from here to Birmingham sour in the barrel and myself three feet off the ground.' 'Gooarn!' said red handkerchief. 'Gidardovit.' 'I certainly can,' he said, beaming all over his face. He stood up straight, folded his arms across his chest, closed his eyes, took a deep breath, and commenced to gabble like a machine gun.

Sure enough very soon he began to rise, very, very slowly at first, as if the floor had some magnetic influence on his feet. Then after the first four inches or so his voice seemed to change into top gear, and his rate of rise speeded up. He achieved the last foot in a matter of a few seconds, and hung there with his eyes closed and completely still save for his lips which jabbered out '...or any kind of ball, bullet, ballast, bomb, ballistic missile, or fissionable explosive material whatever!' Here he finished abruptly, and floated gently back to the floor amid a great ovation.

He silenced us with his arms again, smiling and giving little nodding bows to us all, and continued, 'Yes, gentlemen, if I wished I could talk the rivers up into the mountains and the sea into dry land. I could talk wars lost and won, and all the Kings and Queens of England up out of their graves like jack-in-the-boxes and marching down the streets in purple robes blowing trumpets and kicking the children and shouting for crusaders, and talk Christ risen and recrucified six times a day in every home and factory in England, and talk up the last echo of the last roll of the last drum on the last day of Armaggedon and still talk us all back again without so much as a hair disturbed.' 'Good Heavens,' I said, 'you should stand for parliament.' 'Poof!' he said. 'Why bother? I went to the Houses of Parliament one day and talked myself in and went round all the halls and corridors and lobbies and bars talking and winkling them out of nooks and crannies, and I talked to them all one by one until their ears turned blue and their eyes dropped out, and talked their hair grey and their teeth rotten. I talked them all tired and old and haggard and their joints all stiff, and then I talked their legs from under them and laid them one by one in rows along the corridors and then I talked the windows out and the doors off and talked and talked and talked and talked, until not one stone of the place stood upon another and now only the tourists go there.'

There was an impressed silence for a few seconds, and then a voice said, 'Well, in that case, let's get on with it.'

chapter seven

Brother Knarf bowed politely to both groups of us, then said, 'First of all, then, there are one or two routine formalities to be gone through. Now, to begin with, can I be quite sure that everyone here wishes me to carry out negotiations on his behalf? I wouldn't want to think I was wasting my time, now, would I?' Everyone instantly murmured assent, but I felt that I had to say something here because all this was really nothing to do with me, and in fact I was wasting Brother Knarf's time. I put up my hand, 'No,' I said, 'no, I – er –' A loud boo! went up from the men all round me, and one or two of them punched me on the back and chest. But Brother Knarf instantly silenced them by roaring 'Is this a free country?' to which only one of the men replied by muttering that of course it was but that we could do with a bit more solidarity. Then red handkerchief spoke up quite chirpily. 'If he doesn't want to be represented then it's up to him. Fair's fair. It's a democracy and everybody has to have a free choice because it's a free country and it's up to him to decide.'

All the men in suits clapped and cheered at this and finally everyone agreed that I wasn't on any account to be forced to do anything I didn't want to do. 'Then let us proceed,' said Brother Knarf. 'First of all, of course, there is the little matter of subscriptions.' 'Oh, certainly,' said red handkerchief. 'How much will you need?' 'Oh, as much as you can afford, gentlemen. You understand that nothing can be done without money.' 'We certainly do,' said red handkerchief.

'Come on, boys, stump up.' With that they all started rummaging about in their pockets, while the group on the other side of the room sat silently and watched. I felt very embarrassed, and since I hadn't any money with me anyway, thought that I should say something. I started to explain, as politely as I could, that I really wasn't involved in all this at all and I hoped that they might excuse me if I didn't contribute. But before I could finish a very rough and dirty man grabbed me by the throat and shook me about. He crunched his teeth together and rolled his eyes about independently of one another and said, 'Grooer! You'll be ready enough to reap the benefits, ready enough to take the rises when they come and slip 'em in yer pocket!'

Everyone else in the group growled and they pushed me about, swearing and saying, 'Bloody parasite' and 'layabout'. The nasty man went on, 'We've gotta pull your load for you, I s'pose. People like you ought to be slung out.' The rest of the group growled even more, and one man told me that I should go away and join the group on the opposite side of the room if I wasn't prepared to play my part in this one. 'You go over there, mate,' he said pointing. 'They like people like you over there. You wouldn't get much change out of that lot, you'd be sent to Coventry and no nonsense!' The rest of them roared and growled and poked me about, and said that I should certainly go away and join the other group if that was the way I felt, and they started to push me to my feet. 'Well, I'm not really fussy where I sit,' I said, trying to pacify them. 'If you really think I should go over there I don't mind at all. I'm sure I never meant to be a burden to you.' So saying, I stood up and took a step over the seated men, but they all became angrier than ever, and several of them jumped up and pushed me on to the floor again. 'Cheeky, eh?' said the rough man. 'Desert yer mates, eh? Turn traitor to yer class as quick as kiss yer arse!' The others roared again and swore at me and called me deserter and traitor and blackleg and a host of other nasty things. 'We shall have to send you to Coventry,' spoke up the red handkerchief man. All the others shouted, 'Aye!' and red handkerchief said, 'Right, then, not a word.'

Brother Knarf had meanwhile been borrowing a bowler hat from the other group and now he began to pass it around amongst us. As the money clinked in they all nattered and naggered at me at once, and I felt very uncomfortable. When the hat was full red handkerchief passed it up to Brother Knarf, who emptied the contents into his overall pocket and then strode over to a telephone in the corner and picked up the receiver.

Instantly the door burst open and a great crowd of men carrying pieces of wood and hardboard scrambled in, erected a partition which cut the room in half from corner to corner and floor to ceiling, and left again by the same door. The partition was painted a pinky-blue colour which was neither offensive nor pleasant to the eye and it was completely plain, having no windows, but one door exactly in the middle. Brother Knarf, who had been left in our section, announced that now at last the negotiations would begin. 'I shall go through that door,' he said, 'and I shall whistle up fire from the centre of the earth and winds from all corners of the sky and put collars round their necks. I shall call up all the angels in Heaven and all the devils in Hell and whip them and whack them and press them to your service, and I shall take the sun in my right hand and the moon in my left hand and bang them together until the victory is yours.' So saying he opened the door in the partition, stepped through and closed it behind him.

I thought that now was the time for me to explain my own position and go, but I was shushed very loudly by everybody. They were listening intently. From the other side of the partition a droning voice could be heard, and presently all my companions tiptoed over to the partition, and I could only follow. The droning continued for about ten minutes, and then there was a sound of many men laughing suddenly as if at some joke. Then came a sound like champagne bottles being opened and glasses being filled.

Red handkerchief roared out a blistering curse, knocked the rest of us aside and demolished the door with one blow of his fist. He was sent reeling back, coughing and choking and blinded by a thick pall of smoke which was unmistakably that of expensive cigars. As it began to clear we saw the men standing in a circle in the fug, all listening to Brother Knarf, who had changed his overall for a smart new suit just like the others. He held a fat cigar in his mouth and a glass of something in his hand as did everyone else, and they all looked jolly and agreeable. When they saw us they took the cigars out of their mouths and held their drinks out of sight and looked very solemn. The Brother hurried over to us struggling to get his overall on over his charcoal jacket. He came right through the door, threw his cigar back again and closed the door.

'So!' said red handkerchief. 'You talk now.' 'Certainly,' said the other. 'We were having a little celebration.' 'And what were you celebrating?' 'Why, a settlement, of course!' 'How much?' 'Wait for it,' said Brother Knarf. 'Tuppence farthing a week.' Red handkerchief screwed up his eyes and mouth as if he had been struck in the face, then tipped back his head and howled out a terrible curse. He clenched his fists until the bones cracked. Recovering his composure again he said quietly, 'We are forced to use the last weapon of the working classes. We shall strike!' 'Oh, no,' said the Brother, 'you can't strike.' 'The right to strike,' said the other a little louder, 'is a time-honoured and inalienable working class right.' 'Perhaps it was at one time, my man,' replied Brother Knarf in a voice which was like flicking ash from a cigarette, 'but now you can only strike when I tell you to, which is very seldom, because strikes are very upsetting for everybody. You cannot strike because if you do I shall declare it unofficial, and then you will all be scabs and blacklegs, so there. Besides,' he added, 'if I know anything about anything, you've all got so much stuff on hire purchase, including your houses I shouldn't be surprised, that you've practically surrendered your right to strike anyway. You people are living in the past, you know, they buried Robert Owen a century ago.' I thought that red handkerchief would seize him by the throat then, but the Brother accidentally dropped a piece of paper which he was holding behind his back. One of the men picked it up, but he snatched it back quickly. 'What's that?' demanded red handkerchief, like an executioner who has stopped his axe halfway down. 'My knighthood,' said Brother Knarf, sounding like a child caught with illicit sweets.

Red handkerchief turned blue then, and steam hissed out of his ears. He raised his clenched fists high above his head and would have driven Brother Knarf into the floor like a battering ram, but the Brother started to talk and talk. He quoted figure after figure which proved, he explained, that the financial position of the factory was, while being extremely good, also extremely bad, and finally he ended with the words, '... and as the Prime Minister says, the only way we can have as much as we want is to go without, and I advise you all to make your ways quietly back to your machines, to count your blessings and work as hard as you possibly can.' All the men nodded, turned round and walked quietly out of the door they had first come in by, and I thought it best to follow them.

They would be heading for the lift I thought. I didn't fancy the lift again, or being shut up in it with these men at this particular time. God knows what they might do to each other on the way down, so I turned to the right out of the door, leaving them going straight on. I was sure that the head of a flight of stairs could not be far away. Sooner or later, I was sure I should see one which said 'Stairs', or even 'Stairs down to assembly line', or I should meet someone and could ask the way. I marched on, with my shoes ringing on the shiny wood block floor. I passed a place where a hop-scotch pitch had been marked out carefully in white paint on the floor, and then there was a huge chessboard painted in black and white squares across the whole width of the corridor. Soon after that I was obliged to step over a tennis net, but nowhere could I see any players. I walked on and on.

Presently I thought I saw a small group of people at the far end of the corridor in front of me. They seemed to be standing in a row, but when at last I got to them they were only coats and hats hanging on the wall. I strode on. There was no sound but the hum of machinery far below. I tried to gather from this noise what kind of machinery it was, so that I might have some idea where I was in the factory, but it was only a hum. Perhaps I should hear it better, I thought, if I put my ear to the ground, and so I went down on all fours and did so. The noise did sound a little louder, but it had just occurred to me that I must look very undignified, when I heard a door open immediately behind me. I scrambled to my feet feeling very embarrassed, but determined to enquire the way to the nearest stairway, but before I had reached my feet the door had closed again, and I was alone. I waited, trying to look as dignified as possible in order to counteract the first impression I must have given, but the door did not open again and I heard no noise at all from the other side of it. I knew that someone must be inside. Should I knock and go in and ask the way? I hesitated to do this. There were no notices like 'Do not disturb' or 'Private' on the door, or indeed on any of them; in fact there was no notice or number on this one at all, but that might be because everyone who had proper cause to be in the vicinity was for some reason familiar with this particular door and what lay behind it. The very fact that it bore no message at all might mean that it was actually extra private, a sort of calculated understatement which would of course be more effective than a hundred notices. I wondered what ferocious notices it might have out-valued; but just a little knock, I thought. So I tiptapped very quickly and quietly. No answer, or sound. Should I try again, I wondered ? Again I gave a little tap, perhaps a little louder. Again silence. I shall knock once more, I said to myself, and then if there is no answer I shall walk on, so a third time I knocked. I was rather relieved, I think, when there was still no reply.

I had just turned away from the door when I heard its doorknob rattle. I turned back to the door, but it did not open. The doorknob just went on rattling. I could see it moving a little in a clockwise direction, then back again, and up and down, then anti-clockwise a little way and so on, trembling and rattling all the time. It went on doing this, and after a full half minute I decided that since, having knocked, I could hardly walk away with it rattling like this, I must open the door and see who was trying to open it and if they were doing so in answer to my knock. But the rattling stopped just as I was about to take hold of the knob. I waited for several seconds, then once again forced myself to make a decision. There was silence. No one was answering the door to me. Therefore, I must go away. I must have taken about ten steps down the corridor when the rattling started again. Carry on, for God's sake, said one half of me. I had knocked on the door, and now it was being answered. Was I no better than those ill mannered and inconsiderate little children who are the bane of our streets? Probably some poor weak old man was trying to open it from his bathchair, or, what seemed more likely, someone who was carrying a tray of tea or something. I turned back and ran to the door, but the rattling stopped before I reached it. I grasped the knob firmly and pushed open the door. A large tabby cat strolled out and rubbed itself against my legs. I would have bent to stroke it, but it smelt so foul that I thought I had better be away, having wasted so much time here. I strode off down the corridor, but the cat came bounding after me and rubbed itself against my legs even as I walked, so that I almost tripped. It was like a snake, but I hopped over it and ran a few steps away from it. It seemed to like that and sprang at my left ankle with its claws out, and hung on. One must be polite, I thought to myself, even to cats, if one is to get anywhere at all, so I stopped and bent down to stoke it, but it jumped away to a door which was labelled 'Int. Tox.', stretched up to the doorknob and began to rattle it loudly with its paws. This is nothing to do with me, I thought, and I can hardly go opening doors labelled 'Int. Tox.' just because cats rattle the doorknobs. I hastily walked on, but the rattling went on behind me. Then I thought that perhaps I was responsible after all because I had let the cat into the corridor in the first place, where no doubt it was not supposed to be, and where it annoyed people by tripping them up and rattling doorknobs and smelling, so I stopped.

The rattling went on. The corridor in front of me was very long, I observed, so someone might well put his head out of 'Int. Tox.' and accuse me of meddling with cats and doors before I could turn the corner at the end, and if I sprinted he would probably think I was some kind of burglar and raise the alarm. I should be hard put to it to explain my presence here. Had I to go back, then, and open the door for the animal? A feeling of irritation surged over me. Open a door which I had no business to open and which I did not want to open, in order to let through a stinking cat which did not belong to me and in fact had nothing at all to do with me, which was for all I knew a stray and belonged to nobody and embarrassed everybody? I would not be bullied by such an animal. As if it had sensed my mood, the cat broke out into such a yowling and screeching in addition to the rattling that I lost all my new-found nerve and rushed back to it. A quick flick of the knob, I thought, open the door the width of the cat, in with him, close the door; but the cat would not go in. I tried to push it in with my foot, but it wriggled round. I slipped and the door swung wide open.

I saw before me then a scene of such great charm and dignity that I could not take my eyes from it. Ladies tastefully dressed and gentlemen in fine suits were strolling together or standing in threes and fours. They were smiling and nodding to one another, while some gentlemen were bowing gracefully to ladies who were curtseying elegantly back. One or two couples were dancing a minuet together, the gentlemen holding white handkerchiefs in their left hands and bowing and nodding in a charming way. The whole scene was one of the utmost culture and refinement, so that tears almost came to my eyes. I closed the door quietly and tiptoed on my way. If such people as this, I thought, inhabited this place, then Mr Walpole was right to value so highly the existing order of things. It was worth all the sweat and all the agony of all the rest of us to preserve such a picture. Surely, I thought, if the man in charge of the foundry and the man in the red handkerchief and all the other discontented souls below could see such a sight as I have just seen they would go to work with a ready hand and a light heart, and bear their hardships thankfully.

But still I must speak to someone, and now I was convinced that if I knocked and opened any door I should be received courteously, at least, by these people, so I knocked on another door. There was no answer, so I knocked again and opened it. Inside was another large office. There were men and women all laughing and smiling together and all so obviously enjoying themselves that instantly my heart went out to them and a lump came in my throat. Some of the men were running after the women and pinching them gently on their bottoms, while other men in shirtsleeves were catapulting little paper pellets at others with elastic bands.

Some others were launching paper darts in the air, and everybody was laughing, and the younger women held their hands to their breasts with their delight, as young women sometimes do. I closed the door on them. I could not interrupt, I, a rough workman, breathing on them and speaking in such a place was unthinkable, but I walked on with a lightened step. The culture of China and the glory of Greece were both supported by the toil of anonymous and wretched millions, I thought. So it is with us, and that is how it should be.

I came to another door and knocked. It was not answered, so I opened it quietly to behold a room crowded with naked couples entwined in copulation. Their bodies moved and swayed like the waves of the sea, and the air was full of sighing and whimpering like the sound of doves. They were in all sorts of fantastic and complicated positions amongst the furniture, and many seemed to be expressing their love in very unnatural ways, but with such tenderness and such serenity that questions of propriety seemed out of place. I could only stand and gaze at them as one gazes in a cathedral, or at a sunset from a hilltop. But this was not a cathedral or a hilltop, I said to myself, and where are your manners, Pinquean Smallcreep. I closed the door quietly, and went on my way enveloped in a cloud of singing birds.

Along the corridor towards me came a man in a long white overall gown. He was tall and slim, with the features of a young Athenean. Overflowing with goodwill, I greeted him with enthusiasm. 'Good afternoon,' I said. 'Is it not good to be alive in England at such a time as this?' He looked at me suspiciously. 'It may be,' he said, 'but surely it doesn't merit so much good humour.' 'Ah,' I replied, 'but I have seen such a vision of beauty and joy that I am filled with new hope for all mankind, and if you will open those doors and peep inside you will see for yourself what has so inspired me.' 'What nonsense you talk,' said the man. 'You saw some old paper screens which we hang over the doors to keep the draught away.' 'But they moved,' I protested. 'The draught moves them about,' said the man and strode over to the doors saying that it was time the screens came down because they were old and dusty. He opened all the doors in turn and tore down great sheets of paper from just inside, which he dragged out all crumpled and torn into the corridor.

Then I saw that they were in fact what I had seen, coloured printings on poor quality paper. The man went through one of the doorways, and, looking inside, I saw that all three doors led into one room, the centre of which was occupied by a huge heap of some granular substance. Going closer I saw that it was a heap of money, as big as a house, coins tumbling and notes flying as a number of men spaced out around its edge shovelled the money furiously into sacks and buckets and cardboard boxes, or just shovelled it back as fast as they could. I came closer again, and saw that the money was pouring out of a large pipe which stuck out of the wall, and at such a rate that it seemed to me that the room would soon be filled with money to the ceiling and the men all drowned in it.

A number of men in white coats were rushing round and round the heap urging the other men to shovel faster and trying to hold sacks open for them, but they were so agitated and upset that they only got in the way and made things worse. They were hopping and skipping about shouting, 'Hurry, hurry, oh! how can we be expected to cope!', and making hustling gestures with their arms as if trying to frighten the money back. But it crept forward all the time, halfcrowns and pennies tumbling and sliding down the heap after each other and bowling around on the floor, and pound notes scattering about like leaves. One man was grabbing at the money and stuffing it frantically into his pockets in handfuls and then saying, 'Oh, it's no good!' and flinging it out again. The heap was growing fast, and one man who had been shovelling was up to the waist in it and trying to dig himself out. They would surely drown, I thought, and I ran into the room, picked up a sack and started to fill it by scooping the money up in my hands, but the sack seemed to have a hole in the bottom and the money all came out again. I ran around to find another sack, but all the other men stopped what they were doing and shouted at me that I had no business there and had better clear off before they sent for the police. I tried to explain that I was only trying to help, but they said that there were plenty of people about ready to help out like that, and pushed me out of one of the doors and then slammed all three of them shut.

I felt a little upset by all this and determined to find someone without delay and ask them the way down out of this place into regions with which I was more familiar. The next door I came to was marked 'Sales', which sounded harmless enough, not like 'Meeting Room' or 'Progr.', where one might hesitate to knock for fear of interrupting someone at something terribly important. I knocked, and for once was immediately answered by a deep and sonorous 'Come in'.

Was someone expected, then? Was this to be the beginning of some embarrassing episode of mistaken identity from which it was already too late to extricate myself? I pushed open the door and entered.

chapter eight

I stood before a desk, facing a seated man whose appearance was startling. His nose was long and tapering and needle sharp, and curved down almost to his chin, which came forward to meet it. The skin of his face was powdery white and his eyes were just like white shells set in red leather, and there were black and white lines drawn round them which extended down his nose on each side. His mouth was set in a hideous smile swooping up on each side of his face to his ears, which were blue and purple and which extended downwards in long scarlet lobes like the wattles of a hen. I completely forgot what I had intended to say and stood staring at him, but although speechless I was at the same time angry with myself for appearing to be so ill-mannered, so I said the first thing which came into my head. 'It is my conviction that everything has a rational explanation,' I heard myself say. Not a bad beginning for a conversation, I thought.

His tongue flicked in and out once or twice, and then the smile was pulled even higher up the face. Seeing the hitherto motionless skin move, I was shot through with a ripple of horror, as I am when I see snakes in the zoo move about in their cages by manipulating the surface of their skins. The man looked like some repulsive comedian who might at any moment lift up his trouser legs and take out his kneecaps, or put one leg round his neck and dance some obscene dance on the other. Then the deep voice said, 'It is fortunate for you, and for all of us, that not many people hold such a view.'

Somehow his voice broke the spell, and he didn't look like a snake any more but like a man sitting at a desk smiling at me, and he motioned to me to take a chair which was nearby. 'Surely,' I said, 'This is the age of enlightenment, of science, the age of reason.' I sat down then, and he offered me a cigar which I declined as politely as possible. He leaned over the desk and his face came close to mine. For an instant the feeling of repugnance returned.

'Magic!' he hissed. 'Really?' I said. 'Yes,' he whispered. 'At this present time man has called the dark forces to his aid as never before in his long history, and this age will be looked back on as the age of science, of magic, of unreason. Our Seers, our knowers of the unknown, our adepts of the strange and esoteric arts, our sole mediators to the dreadful forces of the universe – they are our scientists, muttering in workshops, dressed in white robes, speaking in tongues, controlling or releasing storms of fire and tempests of disease.' 'That may be,' I said, 'but the ordinary man in the street doesn't believe in magic. This is the age of the material, of materialism.'

He waved his cigar in a gesture of dismissal. 'A popular fallacy. We have entirely lost touch with the material, and live suspended in a world of ghosts and spirits. Your man in the street rides through his life reclining on a stretcher made of miracles. Compared with ourselves Christ was an amateur conjuror, compared with this factory the jungles of Africa are like Victorian drawing rooms. In the second half of the twentieth century we find the human mind at its most confused, able to be convinced in all its wretchedness that the possession of such-and-such a magic object will give it nobility, in all its weakness that the possession of some other object will give it strength, another beauty, another tranquillity, another virility, another knowledge of and power over the surrounding universe. And when these charms have failed time and time again it is ever ready to start all over again. Today we find the mind at its most frightened. Not rational fears, like the fear of guns or of water – such fears it conquers easily – but a fear which comes of its own new-found awareness.'

He paused to light his cigar by blowing briefly on the end of it, then took a long slow pull which made the lighted end spit and crackle. I fidgeted. 'I tell you,' he went on, 'Hell itself could not contain worse terrors than the ones we live with now. The fact that at any instant the sky might crack open and the earth heave and the trees scream out and this whole country of ours dissolve in fire is but the least of them. Creatures lurk in the corners and cupboards of this factory more dreadful than any which ever inhabited the darkest primordial jungle; faceless, formless, sniggering presences which clutch at the genitals of passing men, or charge men with madness and set them at each other's throats.'

He exhaled a great cloud of cigar smoke and said, 'I see one now, sitting at your shoulder, nibbling at your ear, peeping in your pockets –' Involuntarily I looked round. 'Oh really, come now,' I protested, 'give me more concrete instances.' 'Certainly,' he said, without a pause. 'Throughout the ages men had believed in malignant little spirits which inhabited dwellings, or holes in the ground, or lurked in streams and wells. We have our germ-creatures, who similarly inhabit houses and drains and crevices, or certain specified substances.' 'But germs actually exist,' I said, 'everybody knows that.' 'Have you ever seen one?' he retorted. 'Is it possible to see them?' 'No, I've never seen one,' I admitted, 'but there are people who look at them every day through microscopes.' 'Oh yes,' he said, 'the witchdoctors see them with their magic instruments.' 'But they do,' I explained politely, 'they actually do.' 'Oh, I don't doubt it,' he said in a soothing voice. 'I also do not doubt that witchdoctors are actually aware of evil spirits, probably actually see them. But the modern housewife, who daily performs long and exhausting rituals to exorcise these creatures, has never actually seen one, and it is a simple medical fact that her rituals are irrationally elaborate. All this cleanliness, clean floors to walk on, clean clothes, odourless bodies, children with clean faces, clean cars, even the tops of shoes. Then there is our obsession with whiteness. What could be more irrational than the concepts 'Whiter than white', 'Seven shades whiter' and 'Add brightness to whiteness'? But these ideas sell cleaning powders and sell them to the entire population. Sheets, bread, baths, weddings, collars, crockery and skin, all must be white, because whiteness is believed to be proof against evil influences. You see, we retain in full that irrational preoccupation with appearance rather than with content which is characteristic of the primitive mind. To the savage all that glitters is gold, and with us whiteness is purity, propriety is goodness. We make cars and shoes and teacups shiny, and judge commodities by their wrappings, whether we think we do or not, and men by their clothes.'

Another long pull at the cigar, and he went on, 'As I said, we have entirely lost touch with the material world. Once upon a time, when our lives depended on the cut of a flint or the time of a sowing, every little child knew the feel of a good stone and the habits of the sun, and what you could do and what you couldn't do with an oak sapling, even if spirits did live in them. But the average modern householder hasn't the faintest idea how the polyester-faced pressed wood of his radiogram cabinet got to be like that, and has neither feeling for nor knowledge of the real nature of valves. What man lays his hand on a stone now to hear its heart beat, or thinks of the wind and the water and the fire which turned into rock the bricks of his house and the plates in his kitchen? He only thinks that because the house is strong and permanent it may offset his own feelings of insignificance and transientness, and that if his crockery is invested with a quality of delicacy it will somehow make him less piglike than he knows himself to be.'

He leaned back in his chair and drew on the cigar again. 'We have invented for ourselves,' he continued, 'a complete imaginary world where people do not die but are everlastingly attractive to the opposite sex, where everything is clean, where it is always spring and the streams are menthol-fresh, where everything is exciting, where everyone can be a rebel and a bohemian but at the same time can be clean and smart and surrounded by people exactly like themselves, where everyone is an adequate, self-possessed and civilised human being. I am concerned with selling, and I work here in the knowledge that I am selling magic objects, charms, which transform the owner miraculously into whatever he wishes to be or protect him from things which threaten him.'

I fidgeted. Time was running on. He put both his elbows on to the table and brought his hands together in front of his face. 'If the manager says that things are getting slack, I sit down and think up a new idea. It may be absolutely new, because newness itself is at present considered to be a very powerful magic, and so my imagination may travel all the realms of possibility. I decide on something – say, for instance, woolly jackets for birthday cakes – and set in motion a scheme which will result in a woolly jacket for every birthday cake in England.'

'You couldn't sell woolly jackets for birthday cakes,' I said. 'Oh indeed I could,' he said, 'with no trouble at all. I will briefly outline the campaign for you, if you would like me to.' 'Oh, please don't bother,' I said hastily, but it was too late. 'No bother at all. Now, first of all I have to put the idea into its Function Category. There are three function categories, the Defecative, the Projective, and the Defacative-projective. Ideally all consumer objects should come in the last category, but in practice few do. Now, woolly jackets for birthday cakes quite definitely belong to the first, the Defecative, that is they have the power to protect from or cancel out evil influences or threatening presences. The threatening presences which particularly concern us here are the unborn children of a man's wife. All men are subconsciously threatened by their unborn children. They know that it is theoretically possible for their wives to conceive once every month, and they see these conceptions stretching away into the future endlessly, like the endless diminishing reflections in two opposing mirrors. The awareness of this massive army of little people haunts married men day and night and can affect them in many unpleasant ways, not the least of which may be to render them impotent towards their wives. One way out which is open to them is to eat.'

'I don't quite follow,' I said, twirling my thumbs round and round each other in my lap. 'I should hardly expect you to,' he said, smiling. 'But we who have studied these things have found out, amongst all the other things which we have found out, that there is a strong association in the human subconscious between eating and destroying one's enemies. This reaches the most literal expression in cannibalism, but it has many manifestations which are only a little less obvious in our own society. When a housewife opens her oven, takes from it a cake and places it before her husband for him to eat, and when this cake is furthermore a birthday cake, there can be no doubt that not all the enthusiasm with which he cuts it up and eats it can be attributed to its flavour, however fine.'

'Well, it all sounds perfectly harmless to me,' I said, wondering how much longer he would go on. 'Oh, indeed it is,' said he, 'but unfortunately the matter does not end there. For, you see, this poor man doesn't really like to think that he's the kind of fellow who would carve his children up and eat them, unborn or not, and this sets up a conflict – all below the level of his consciousness, of course, in his poor mind. Thus we can say that not all his refusals to eat the cake which his wife has cooked can be attributed to his bad digestion or to the fear that his wife may poison him. More often than not they are the result of feelings of guilt and remorse. However, he both fears his unborn sons and likes cake, and this is where I come along to help him. "If you were first to show respect and concern for your children, if you were to carry out some act to prove to yourself that you are the good and loving father which you have always believed yourself to be, where then can the harm be in eating a bit of birthday cake?" However, I do not say it in so many words. I would have a poster displayed which would depict a man with his mouth open wide, holding a piece of birthday cake. The unwritten message would read "Has that birthday cake been properly looked after since it left the oven? Has it been lying in a cold cake tin? Was it just put down on a cold hard plate and left there?" and then the punch line – "You can only enjoy that cake properly if it has been kept warm and snug in a Bongo Woolly Cake Jacket, obtainable at any good outfitters, price such and such.'"

He leaned back in his chair in triumph, while I felt as if I had just walked over a mountain. 'Is it really as simple as that?' I said. 'It really is,' he beamed. 'People can, with a little prodding in the right places, be persuaded to buy anything, eat anything, join anything, believe anything, vote for anybody, or do anything you like to think of. In Britain today we persuade people to spend most of their waking lives doing work they hate, spend most of their money on things they don't need, rear children they don't want and force them to acquire an education which is useless to them; live with women they've grown tired of, vote for politicians they know nothing about, respect people who sponge on them, help to enforce laws which rob them of what is rightfully theirs, give their faithful support to unions which tie their hands behind them, and do all sorts of things you wouldn't think possible.'

'Really,' I said, more to keep myself awake than anything. He continued, 'We persuade people to swear by one particular brand of a dozen identical makes of cigarette, to favour passionately one of three negligibly differing political parties, we persuade them to worship one swindler and hate another, bow down to one layabout and spit on another, worship and obey one madman and lock up another, salute mass murderers and hang men who kill their wives, and in general simultaneously hold contradictory or diametrically opposing opinions about any human act, attitude or posture. People like yourself are allotted both the worst jobs and the least money, and are persuaded that that is the very quintessence of justice.'

I smiled and nodded politely and said, 'Very interesting,' and then, 'I really think I must be getting along now, sir, if you will forgive me,' and I stood up. 'Oh yes, certainly,' he said. 'You must pop up and have a chat with the managing director now you're here,' and he pressed a button on his desk.

I protested that I wouldn't be so presumptuous as to take up the time of such a man. 'Oh, nonsense,' he honked. 'He's very glad to talk to anyone, he's a lonely old man up there.'

Straightaway there appeared a naked woman who would have been attractive enough fully dressed. She wore blue flowers in her hair and tiny bows of red ribbon tied into her pubic hair. Her lips were the brightest red, and her nipples were painted to match and bobbed prettily as she walked. Her body was not as thin as I believe it is currently fashionable for women's bodies to be, but swelled and hummocked with the generosity of an inflated rubber dinghy. Her lips and breasts and buttocks were like bursting fruits, her belly was more than anything like an overcambered road, with a bottomless navel like bath water running out. She was formed like gently drifting snow over tussocks of grass, like thick warm custard over cherry pie. The salesman said something, I forget what, and I followed this creature across the office, forgetting, as far as I can remember, to so much as say goodbye to him. Her back trembled and rippled as she walked, the dimples winked at me alternately from either side of her buttocks. The backs of her knees were incredibly exciting, each one was like a naked woman itself, perfect, symmetrical, without a crease. I should have been content to have one of those alone to do as I pleased with. Looking at her now my body ached from head to foot as it had never ached before, and I felt as if I carried a sack of coal suspended between my legs. She took me to a door, opened it, turned like a dream to let me pass through. As I did so my upper arm brushed one of her breasts, and I thought that it had burned my sleeve. Then she shut the door behind me, and I never saw her again.

I sat down on a step and bowed my head in pain, and remembered what it had felt like to want a woman for the first time and without hope. The cold occasional wheezing winter streetlamps came back to me, the loneliness of wet streets around a particular house, the desolation of wet slate roofs in rows, and coal smoke falling into windless empty streets with shiny pavements. I remembered the sound of footsteps faintly rounding the far corner and trot-trotting glistening umbrellas into view, and then passing the house, and passing me, and fading away along Acacia Road into silence. Cold dripping silence, broken only occasionally by cars with hissing tyres bursting across the end of the road from left to right, or from right to left, while my feet got colder and my back got wetter and nobody stirred at the house. The lighted windows would begin to vanish one by one, and then a dark man riding a bicycle and carrying a long pole would whistle and hiss his way down the street putting out the lamps one after the other and folding up the night behind him, and extinguishing the last hope. The fields came back to me, flat endless Essex fields, cold leafless ploughed winter fields under dead grey skies, uninhabited, uninhabitable, leaching out warmth from any part of the body exposed, even from between two joined hands, and boredom clogging round our feet and stuffing our mouths.

I pulled myself together and stood up. I was standing at the bottom of a steep flight of spiral stone stairs, which had no rail. The impression was of a monastery, and contrasted with the warmth and colour of the place I had just left. I began to climb and found the steps spiralling very tightly indeed so that I couldn't feel my feet and felt as if my head was a complete revolution ahead of them. I became breathless and the stairs became dark. I rested, leaning against the hard stone outer wall, with the central column of the stairway coming up between my legs swinging the stairs around it like a football rattle. Up again, and then at last a door, with a faded notice pinned to it. I knocked, and a tired voice asked me to come in.

I creaked open the door to see a large man, in a small room which looked more like a prison cell than a managing director's office. He sat in a swivel chair which was the only piece of actual furniture in the room, with his paunch easing its way over his trousers. He was the saddest looking man I have ever seen; sadness weighed down great pouches from his eyes and cheeks and throat like loops of wet fishing-net, and a face so limp and long that it hung down to his waist. It wore a damp and kindly smile, however, and the butterflies which had been in my stomach vanished. The room contained a small chair with its lining hanging out and two old oil drums, upon one of which sat a telephone and on the other an ancient typewriter.

'Good afternoon,' he said in a sad damp voice which sounded as if it had once boomed and resonated, but now it was worn and tired, and cracking like the voice of an old man. I said good morning, but didn't know what to say next. He rescued me by motioning me towards the chair and saying, 'I hope that you will forgive me for what I am about to do. I so seldom have the opportunity of speaking to real live people in the flesh in this age of television and radio that I cannot waste time in polite conversation. I wish to make a speech to you.'

Inwardly I groaned, but said, 'It will be a great honour, sir,' and sat down on the chair, which was lumpy. He stood up then, with some difficulty, and I saw that he was eight feet tall. He lumbered into the centre of the room looking at the ceiling. He began to speak as if to an audience in a great theatre.

'Although I know it to be a very great honour to sit at the head of so distinguished a company, and although I would not have it otherwise, it is not without some reluctance and disquietude that I sit here in the capacity of your managing director. I am a lonely and tired old man, whose bones are heavy with the knowledge of sad things, and I hope that you may forgive me for trying to relate some of these things to you, in order that I may thereby be eased. May I go on?'

'Certainly,' I said, resigning myself to yet more delay.

'In the past,' he boomed, 'our captains of industry have earned for themselves the most unenviable of reputations, and I would not hesitate to say that the blame for a not insubstantial proportion of human misery, yes, and of the bloodshed of the last hundred years must rest squarely upon the shoulders of those whose lineage I have chosen to inherit. But lonely as I am, and aware as I am of the fallacy of the concept of human progress, it has been my last untarnished hope that that minority of men about whose shoulders the cloak of true wisdom has come to fall has from age to age increased both in number and in quality of men; for if it is not so I know, and the very knowledge weighs heavily upon me, that the story of man will henceforth be one of retreat, slow but inexorable retreat, into darkness, chaos, terror and despair. Sir, against that retreat only I and such rare men stand, sole guardians of all that is of the essence of civilisation and human culture.'

He paused, and cleared his throat. I felt as if I should offer him a sponge or towel or glass of water or something, but there were none handy and anyway he seemed to have completely forgotten about me, and to be addressing some great crowd below us. He began again sadly in a voice which wrung its hands. 'I must tell you many painful truths, and I shall begin with the truth concerning our product here, the fruit of all your labours. After much deliberation I am forced to the conclusion that its consumption does not, and indeed will not ever, give the satisfaction which has been attributed to it. Its effect is pathetically shortlived, and moreover for most purposes it could be manufactured by anyone in his own home, for we are not magicians, however much we might seem to be. Neither can our product be further improved in any significant way.'

He drew himself up again, and switched on the booming once more. 'Sir, I could not stand before you with such singleness of heart, talking to you of wisdom and of truth, if my only concern were simply the numismatical enrichment of those, however worthy, who work within this great establishment. I speak in the knowledge that, useless as it is, our product is the very lifeblood of our society, and that without its constant and increasing consumption our factory would grind to a halt and the blood-red rust which would corrode our machines would likewise corrode the souls of men and women. Then the retreat into despair, into the universal darkness from which living matter has taken so long to drag itself, would begin, and I believe that that retreat might be swift once it had begun, and that it would engulf us all. Sir, I ask you to believe that twenty years proved of lying and deceit could not shake one quarter of the justification of things being just as they are.' At this he buried his head in his hands as he stood, and I felt most embarrassed. Surely I could not presume to go and comfort the managing director, yet surely I could not sit here and watch a man so sorrowful?

He began again in a tearful voice, crying out as if for forgiveness. 'I am here not because I am particularly qualified to be here, and not particularly because I was chosen or elected, but because I made up my mind to get here. Men who stop bolting horses or save their children from burning houses are not chosen or elected. I came here by all the devices of dishonest argument, by rhetoric, bad promises, meaningless slogans, twisted statistics, proof by selected instances; I was carried here by trumped-up personalities and paid publicity agents, by carefully calculated exploitation of the prejudices, the short memories, the emotions, the selfishness and the general gullibility of the majority of you. I was brought here by methods borrowed from the fairground cheapjack and the circus ring master.'

He gave a short bitter staccato sob, and went on, 'If you prevent men from seizing and wielding power over you by force, you do not solve the problem of human freedom. You merely make it necessary for others to acquire power over you by some other means, for you are no more capable of managing your own affairs than you were before. This vast hollow structure of a democracy is built upon the heads of men and women of whom the majority are no less stupid, no less apathetic, no more concerned with what goes on outside their own small circles than men anywhere. But you wear this great hat, this great expensive elaborate tottering ill-fitting uncomfortable carnival hat, all decked out with plastic flowers and tinsel and little bells, because it makes you feel good, feel cultured and civilised and Greek and superior, in spite of your hydrogen bombs in a world where men loot and kill as much as they ever did, and women and children starve in unprecedented numbers, and in a universe as cold and hostile and meaningless as it ever was.' He paused. 'But graceful hats do not give their wearers grace, neither are dainty hats of any use to whores.'

He bowed his head in sorrow and turned away from me. I was completely puzzled by all this, first of all because I understood little of it, and secondly because I understood enough to know that I was being blamed for all the alleged folly of all my fellow countrymen, which hardly seemed just. He swung round suddenly, his eyes wide with indignation. He pointed at me. 'You are so coy, under your hats,' he burst out. 'Like virgins. You blush and turn away from my advances, feign horror at my intentions, you have to be wooed with fancy boxes and promises of fine clothes.' He shook his head. 'It is as well that the will to power is a strong one.' He stopped and turned sideways to me again. 'But when at last you give yourselves to me I find you panting for me to have my way with you like the bawdiest of barmaids, I find you as lusty and resourceful as myself, and presently you rebuke because I do not handle you roughly enough, or dominate you enough, or use enough imagination in these things. If I did not resist it we should eventually plumb the depths of human indecency, become necrophiles together and walk hand in hand through charnel houses and execution chambers, or write marriage vows on parchment made from human skins, or copulate in burial pits by the light of pyres.'

At this, to my profound embarrassment, he burst into tears, but at length I stood up and went over to him. He stood stooped and quaking there, and I felt an impulse to put my arm round his shoulders, but he was the managing director and I could not. 'There, there,' I said, 'I'm sure everybody loves and respects you, sir.' He blubbered, 'You would prefer an iron-handed dictator to a helpless old man like me.' 'Goodness gracious me no, sir,' I said with conviction. 'Indeed we would not. Why ever should we? Nobody likes a dictatorship, that's common knowledge.' At this he straightened up like a ramrod and roared out as if in terrible agony, 'That is the dreadful fallacy!' I was so startled that I scuttled off to my seat, but he followed me like a lame bull, and turned me round and glowered at me while holding my lapels. He shouted, 'Why, you would kiss the ground he trod, Smallcreep. He would be brutal and greedy and ambitious and lusty, and he would come like a Christ to vindicate you. You would thrill to his speeches, Smallcreep, and you would hear more about justice and freedom, yes, and democracy in one of them than you would hear from me in a lifetime.' He shook me. 'There would be brass bands and patriotism and honour and glory and cheer upon cheer. Service, duty, dedication, heroism, comradeship, adventure and conquest.'

He let go of me then, pushed me back in the chair and stood over me with his paunch near my face. He waved his arms about and shouted, 'You would march behind his flag in shining uniforms, each one of you a prince. You would be men indeed, men of purpose, captains of history, gods to tell the sun when to rise and set.' He turned away from me and ambled across the room with his hands in his pockets. 'And then,' he went on, 'if things went wrong, the whole lot of you would point at him and say, "He made us do it."' He threw back his head and hyenaed. '"He made us do it", you would say, when the whole nation of you had cheered him on, when the saluting arms had covered acres and acres and acres where he had passed. The young men who had strutted like peacocks in their first uniforms would say, "It was all him, he made us do it," and the man next door who's polite to your children, and your mate at work who tells you dirty jokes, who flogged and gassed and tortured, brimming over with patriotic fervour and joy, they would say, "It was him, he was a madman."' He arrived at his chair, turned and slumped into it as if he had come to pieces, his head falling forward like a broken doll. 'In all countries,' he said, 'and at all times in history this dreadful image persists – of a crowd of people cheering and bowing down and obeying one man. It has always signified the utmost evil, it is the very essence of evil.'

I tried to comfort him: 'But didn't we fight for freedom? We would fight for it again!' He did not burst out again, but merely closed his eyes and sagged a little more, as if I had heaped something on to him. 'I do not doubt your ferocity. But one look at freedom, and you would all shrivel up like worms in a snowstorm.' He leaned forward then, as if becoming just a little interested after all in what he was saying. 'You would oscillate between the most intense boredom and the extremity of fear.' He opened his eyes, but not, it seemed, to see out. 'Every week I give you a pay packet, with which you can buy, if you wish, at least a little freedom. But none of you chooses to cash it in that way – you exchange it for families and television and washing machines, and come back next week for more slavery. You do not buy freedom because you dare not. In a society of free men you would be forced to face up to the truth of what you really are. In every sense of the expression you would have to do your own dirty work, you would have to forge your very own relationships with those around you.'

He beckoned to me then, and bent down to the floor and pulled on an iron ring. A trapdoor came up. He motioned me to look down. I did so, and I was looking into some kind of office where half-a-dozen or so men in dark suits sat at desks. These desks were ranged in a circle around a figure in overalls who was crawling on his hands and knees on the floor picking up small objects and putting them in a tin. The office workers, I then noticed, were all smoking cigarettes and seemed to be smoking them as fast as they could, fumbling in packets and lighting each one on the stump of its predecessor before throwing the latter on the floor. 'Listen,' said the managing director.

I could hear swearing and argument, and putting my head a little closer to the trapdoor I heard one of the office workers say indignantly, 'How on earth can we be expected to work properly with all this mess of cigarette-ends on the floor?' and then distinctly, 'Why can he never get the floor clean, the lazy oaf?' All the other men at the desks were grumbling away in the same kind of way, and throwing down the cigarette-ends as fast as they could, while the man on the floor crawled about at great speed picking them up. I heard his deep voice saying, 'The dirty bastards, how can I be expected to keep the floor clean when they keep on throwing fag ends down?', and he was grubbing the little white objects into his tin as fast as he could, gloating over them sometimes, and, I fancied, trying to count them, but he never had time. As we watched I saw him take out another tin and hastily close the first, which was so full that he only managed it after some difficulty, after which he was obliged to scuttle round even faster because the stubs had by then accumulated and the abuse of the office workers had grown louder. He in his turn grumbled more loudly, saying, 'How on earth can I be expected to keep up with such filthy pigs?' The smokers replied by opening their desks and bringing out more packets of cigarettes and boxes of matches, which they stuffed into their pockets, saying, 'The lazy oaf, the filthy floor,' and so on.

The managing director closed the trapdoor and stood up, and I returned to my chair. He paced about a little and began again, 'You are all like our magistrates, who condemn men to prisons they themselves have never lived in, like company directors who haven't the slightest idea of what it is like to work on a production line, like old ladies shovelling coal on to their fires without the faintest glimmer of what it is like to go down a mine and dig out the coal. You are all each other's jailers. You keep a dustbin and then condemn a man to whom you are a complete stranger to spend his days coping with your dirt and refuse. Goodness knows he hates the job, who wouldn't, so you have to say to him, as they do in jails, that if he doesn't do as you wish you will give him nothing but bread and water.' 'He should get a better job,' I said, crossing my legs the other way. 'There are plenty about.' 'But somebody must empty your dustbin, Mr. Smallcreep. If not him, then someone else, or no doubt there would be a great commotion with you at its centre. Likewise, when you buy food you oblige a man to go out into the fields to grow it for you. Buy any manufactured article and you condemn, or, if you like, blackmail, or bribe, a man to spend his waking hours in a factory. All these people in their turn will condemn you to waste your life perhaps in some office or at some other machine, doing for them what you have prevented them from doing for themselves. In a free society, however, you would have no such claims over complete strangers. They would help you if they felt like it, if you were a particularly generous-natured or endearing person. But if you were not then you would have to empty your own dustbin, and dispose of your own sewage, and cure your own sickness. In a free society you would have to come to terms with yourself and with others like yourself, with the man who backs his car into yours, with the man next door who has to feed three times as many mouths as you do, with the drunks who get into your garden. You would have to sort things out with them yourself, instead of having social workers or political parties or policemen or shop stewards to do the job for you, and in the process you would be forced to face up to what sort of a person you yourself really were.'

He paused then, and came over towards me, leaning forward. He went on, 'All your damned courts of law and prisons and all the pompous nonsense by which what you call law and order is maintained, they are not there to protect you from a few psychopaths and criminals. They have been instituted in order that the bulk of citizens can be kept from each other and thus need never come to terms with their own rotten and disordered natures. To meet a murderer in the street is bad, and one may well carry a gun as a precaution. But to meet oneself in the street would be so appalling a nightmare that men sacrifice half their wealth gladly to avoid it. You invest in kings and judges and policemen and equip whole armies at enormous cost. The latest device by which you propose to protect yourselves from yourselves is an invention which will destroy you all completely. You may call such cocktails by fancy names like National Socialism, or Communism, or Democracy, but there is very little freedom in any of them.'

I was amazed by this, coming from a managing director. I declared staunchly and stoutly that we would never tolerate anything resembling Communism or Fascism in Britain. 'Of course not,' he replied. 'You would hang an old woman from every lamppost in London to stamp them out. In the name of anti-fascism you would put into power the most brutal dictator you could find, in the name of anti-communism you would submit to martial law for the rest of your lives.' I was dismayed, 'I most respectfully wish –' I began. 'Go on,' he said in a voice so tired I hardly heard it. 'We have freedom of speech,' I said.

He opened his eyes round and wide and said, 'Oh? Do you frequently make speeches? Do you go to Hyde Park Corner to watch the buffoons?' 'We are great talkers,' I said. 'Oh yes, and no doubt a list of the subjects which you discuss amongst yourselves at work and at home would be a very long one. But then you all take daily newspapers and you know nothing. You do not use words for communication at all, you use them to reinforce herd feelings, you talk for the same reason as sheep bleat and hens cluck. You cannot speak freely because you cannot think freely –' Forgetting myself I protested, 'We all have our own opinions, in a democracy we have a right to our own opinions.' 'Opinions?' he shouted, and got up from his chair. 'You do not know what the word means! You mean that you have a right to your own prejudices, and that is another proposition altogether.' He turned away and wandered sadly over to the typewriter and poked at one or two of the keys.

'Smallcreep, do you not agree,' he said carefully, after a pause, 'that all this talk of freedom of speech and freedom of thought is just so much hogwash and fiddle-faddle if it is not accompanied by freedom of action. Now you cannot have freedom of action because –' Again I interrupted, protesting that of course we had freedom of action. 'This is a free country,' I said, 'everybody knows that.' At this he turned on me, clenching his fists and roaring, 'Then what the devil am I here for? The tourists?' 'But with the greatest possible respect, sir,' I said, determined to make my point, 'it is the freely chosen aim of us all to avoid behaviour which would prejudice the well-being of the community. Most of us are hard working law abiding respectable citizens and wouldn't wish to be otherwise.'

He turned to me with an unpleasant sarcastic sort of smile on his face. 'You see, my dear Smallcreep, the product is always the same. That is just what the average dictator would require you to be, for all his brass bands and uniforms.' 'But we aren't forced to come here at bayonet point,' I said. 'What does it matter as long as you come? You hate your work and yet you all do the overtime I allow you to do. Bayonets or not, the work is no better.' 'But we aren't forced to work hard by you,' I protested. 'Very likely you are underworked,' he shrugged, 'but that is just as bad for you. On the other hand your actual output is very high, and that is a matter of efficient production methods, which are not confined to democracies. In fact, efficiency is one important characteristic of modern totalitarianism.' 'Then we live well,' I said quite impatiently. 'If you mean that you eat well, then I must agree, but that has nothing to do with democracy either, and pigs and horses eat well if their owners have any sense. If you are speaking, however, of the quality of your daily lives, then I do not agree. You are as stultified as tinned sardines, living in a dream world because your real world is so utterly unfulfilling.' 'We are happy,' I flung in as a last attempt to comfort him. He shook his head slowly. 'If a pig in a sty tells you he is happy, what do you think? That he doesn't know what happiness is, of course. The product, Smallcreep, is always the same – a pig who dreams that he is a god.'

All this sounded very confusing and depressing to me, but it was certain that whatever the managing director said was true. I therefore sat on the chair looking sadly down at my feet (which were, I noticed, turned inwards towards one another), trying to find some kind words which might comfort the poor man, who looked as if he might burst into tears yet again. 'I am sure that all these things are true,' I said, 'but they only serve to intensify my own already strong feelings of gratitude and comfort that we should have such a wise and far-seeing man as yourself in authority over this establishment, and I am sure that there is not one decent respectable man here who does not respect and applaud your authority.' 'Save myself,' said the manager, taking out a handkerchief and dabbing sadly at his eyes, 'for there, Smallcreep, you have hit upon the lowest piece of humbug of all. The simple truth is that there is no justification for the authority of one man over another which will stand up to the briefest examination. The whole idea of authority is humbug. I might be leading you all to Hell for all you know.'

'Your authority comes from common consent,' I said. 'Surely that is enough. You were put in this position of power because you are considered by us to be entirely honourable and supremely intelligent and can, therefore, be relied upon to act in the best possible way in any circumstances which may arise,' I said, feeling sure that would cheer him up.

'Considered by you?' he said mockingly, raising his eyebrows. 'If you are all too blind to see the way, how shall you judge if I can see it any better? If you could judge me then I should have no authority at all, because you would be as well able to see as I was. The fact is that you do not know me, have never met me, would be incapable of assessing my qualities anyway. You do no more than vote for an agreeable face or image. I was put here, so Crabb the sales manager tells me, because I had more hair than the other contestants. Supposing that I was entirely honourable and supremely intelligent: both may serve the utmost evil, have frequently and recently done so, have caused enough pain and bloodshed, one would have thought, to teach you a thousand times over that it was so. Do you not understand that the idea of authority and the idea of individual conscience and responsibility cannot exist side by side in the same society, and that, in so far as you have given me authority to make moral decisions for you, you have denied the very principles by which you put me here? Do you not see that the instant I exert my authority on any one of you I destroy the justification of consent? Authority by consent is a contradiction, without consent is merely brute force.'

I began to protest, but he exploded suddenly, splaying out his huge fingers in a gesture of appeal. 'Look at me, man,' he shouted, and to my astonishment he stripped off his jacket and dropped his trousers down as quick as a wink, and stood in his shirt and his sock suspenders. His paunch was large and drooped sadly like the rest of him, and his legs were ridiculously thin to support such a weight, like birds' legs, with big lumpy knee-joints. His flesh was of the colour and texture of uncooked pastry, and bristle-haired in a halfhearted sort of way. 'I am just an old man,' he shouted, 'an old man with a pot belly and a bent back. Toothless,' he ejaculated, and spat out his teeth into his hand and sucked his cheeks and lips inwards. Then, putting his teeth back again, he went on, 'My birth was just as undignified and messy as anyone else's, and caused a frightened woman just as much pain and inconvenience as your own did. I was as helpless and as incontinent and as stupid and as smelly then as everyone else is. I pissed in my bed, Smallcreep, just as you did, I stole and ate green apples and was sick. I have the same appetites and the same needs as any man, I eat and I excrete, and when I go to bed I put on striped pyjamas. Hurt with the same weapons, subject to the same diseases, healed by the same means. Have I supernatural powers? Am I immortal? Have I a jewel set in my forehead?'

I felt as if I should say something like, 'For God's sake pull your trousers up and stop blubbering, man,' but of course I could not do such a thing. But then, as if he read my thoughts, he closed his trembling mouth and pulled up his trousers quickly. He glanced around him as if someone might be watching him, then strode over to me and took me by the throat and shook me. The flesh of his face quivered and shivered in front of my eyes, and his breath came in sobs. 'Say nothing,' he hissed at me, 'nothing of these things to anyone, for if you spread them about you will have every man and woman here quivering with terror in their beds. If there are no justifications for my authority then it is necessary to invent some. I have told you too much, Smallcreep.' I assured him that I hadn't really understood much of it anyway, at least, not enough to be able to relate it to anyone else. 'Anyway, it doesn't concern me,' I said. He seemed satisfied by this, and let go of my throat and turned away.

chapter nine

Suddenly so old and weary that he could scarcely walk, the manager, in answer to my request for directions to the assembly line, took me out on to a landing and told me to wait for two men who would shortly pass, and follow them.

Presently two smart young men came striding along side by side, leaning forward with a look of urgency, gusting along so that their jackets flapped behind them. Under one arm each carried a sheaf of papers, and they nodded and murmured to each other earnestly. 'Here,' I thought as they approached, 'are men with a sense of purpose, men who know where they are going. How wise and helpful of the manager to put me in their charge!' and I fell in behind them feeling confident that my search was near its end. They began to clip-clop down the stairs at a great rate, leaning forward even further like ski-jumpers in flight. I hurried behind them clutching at the stairrail, and found it difficult to keep up with them. Soon I was breathing heavily, and began to realise that I was a great deal older than I had thought. Many years had passed by, I reflected, without my noticing them. But when a man's life becomes, after marriage, strictly regular, a continually repeated daily pattern punctuated by regular weekly and yearly events, it is possible to slip suddenly, as a gramophone needle may jump across the grooves: you may put away your reading or your writing to comfort your children and suddenly find, after you have put them down again, that you are eleven years older. You may go to the factory in the morning thirty-one years of age and come back the same night to find that you are thirty-eight. Sometimes it is only a few days – when you say to your wife, 'Is it Monday or Tuesday today?' and she replies that it is Thursday, or on a particularly cold day you cannot remember if spring is on the way or summer just finished; but when it is years, when you wake up one morning before your wife and find her looking old and sallow beside you, when your children suddenly become pregnant – why, then, it is unpleasant, like recovering from amnesia or waking in a strange room, and you struggle to remember, to fix some event in those years by which they may be reclaimed. But often there is nothing, only identical repetitions of work and home and sleep, and you can only hope that time won't play too many tricks like that.

'Hurry up,' shouted back one of the young men, 'for those who can't keep up will surely get left behind.' I tumbled along behind them as fast as I could, using both my hands on the stair rails to prevent myself falling. 'I'm sorry,' I said breathlessly, 'I am very tired, I have had a long day.' 'Why, what time did you get up in the morning?' said the other young man over his shoulder. 'Oh, I get up at half-past six every morning, but I didn't mean that –' 'Good gracious me!' exclaimed the first as he skipped down the stairs. 'Whatever do you get up at that time for?' 'To get to work,' I replied, concentrating on every step, for I was determined not to lose them. He asked me if I lived a long distance away from the factory, and when I replied that I lived in the town he asked me what time I came to work. 'At 7.45,' I said, and he said, 'Good heavens, whatever for?' I told him that everyone in the workshops started work at that time. 'Nonsense,' he said 'everyone knows that work begins at nine. You manual workers are always making up tales like that.' I didn't like to contradict him, and when the other man asked, by way of making conversation, exactly where I lived, I gladly forgot the other thing and told him. But the first man, who I fancied was the elder of the two, said 'Nonsense' again, and said that there were no houses in that area to his knowledge. I politely explained that there were a number of recently built council houses there.

We had reached the bottom of the stairs, to my great relief, and at my mention of council houses they both stopped on the last step and looked up at me. 'Are you a councillor, then?' they said, with a new tone in their voices. 'No,' I replied, not understanding. They looked at each other briefly, and then leapt off the bottom step like stags. I strode after them and found it a little easier to keep up on the level.

We were walking through a shop where large pipes came down out of the ceiling, and men were holding sacks under the mouths of these pipes while the sacks filled quickly. As each sack was filled the man would heave it up on to his shoulder and stagger away, the sack wriggling and squeaking and heaving about so much that some of the men could scarcely keep them on their shoulders. The younger of the two again spoke. 'I imagine that it doesn't take many minutes from there in the car,' he said, I supposed by way of making polite conversation. 'I have no car,' I said. 'Very few of the married men in the workshops have.' 'Nonsense,' ejaculated the older man again, 'everyone in England has a car today, I can give you statistics to prove it. I could forgive you working-people for grumbling, but when you tell lies as well I lose patience.' But I must not lose patience, I told myself; but I could not resist repeating that I had no car, and that only factory-workers whose wives went out to work could really afford them. I was struck suddenly with an unfamiliar thought about this: all these years I had borne the boredom and waste of spending most of my waking life in the factory, in the belief that I was supporting something of infinite worth – my family, and their home life, in which I was able to take part myself for some of the time. But these working couples who had no children, they worked as many hours as

I did but there was nothing to support. They did not save for some planned future family: from what I knew of most of them I gathered that they spent most of the money, and lived expensively.

As if reading something of my thoughts the older man said, 'No car? You must have a considerable amount invested if you are so frugal.' He then said that he was thinking of buying some new shares and what did I recommend? Thinking that he must be talking about savings, I said, 'I have a small account with the Post Office.' 'The Post Office?' he said. 'Is it possible to buy Post Office shares?' His friend said that I probably meant some kind of government stock, and he looked disgusted at this, 'You people have no courage, no enterprise.'

We were now hurrying through a workshop full of machinery. The men pressed forward so fast that I fancied that the machines on either side of us swayed slightly with the force of our passing, opening a little and then closing behind us in a kind of wave. Also the roof was booming about again, and I could plainly see it lifting and falling high above us in some fearful gale up there. I became quite frightened, and said to the two men in front, 'I think there is something wrong with the roof.' But the noise of the machinery must have drowned my voice, for they took no notice and only hurried on, little eddies of dust catching at their heels.

Presently we entered another section, where more men were filling sacks from the mouths of great pipes, and I noticed that these sacks were all alive and wriggling too. I noticed several things which made me think that this might be the same shop, but dismissed the idea until we entered the next department, which was, as before, a workshop full of various kinds of machinery, where I became convinced that we had somehow missed the way and come in a circle. The men were moving even faster now, it seemed to me, and the machinery swayed quite alarmingly as we passed. 'I'm sure we've only just been through here,' I shouted above the noise of the machinery, but they did not hear. Again I heard the distant booming, and again the roof was billowing about. I hurried as fast as I could, trying to keep up close behind them. The machines were sliding in behind us as the sea closes in behind a ship, and suddenly there was a great crash and I looked behind us to see that a huge multiple mill as big as a house had toppled over into the gangway in our wake. 'A machine has fallen over,' I shouted, but the only reply I got was, 'Nonsense, hurry up now.'

Out of the machine shop we sped and into a sack-filling shop again, which I was quite certain was the same one. I shouted out that there could be no doubt that we were walking in a circle, but they only called back, 'Save your breath' and, 'You people are always looking for things to grumble about.' Into the machine shop we swept again, and there ahead lay the mill, lying on its side in the gangway. 'There you are,' I shouted, 'that's the mill. That proves we've passed this way already.' 'On the contrary,' replied the older man as we squeezed under the mill, 'since we have not passed this mill before it proves that we have not been this way already,' and they bounded away with their ties waving over their shoulders. I ran to keep up, with my head down pressing against the wind. I heard behind us another crash and another and then the booming of the roof, and I shouted, 'The factory is crumbling, what can we do?' The answer came, 'Press on, press on and don't talk nonsense!' As we came rushing into the sack-filling department again I shouted, 'Stop, stop, I must rest, please wait,' but they only shouted, 'Nonsense, nonsense,' and 'Those who can't keep up get left behind.'

I stopped then, and sat down to recover my breath. Within a few seconds they were out of sight. I could rest and pick them up when they came round again; but if they really were walking in circles what would be the use of following them? I waited, if only for the satisfaction of proving to them that I was right, but they did not come, although I rested for a long time. Perhaps I was wrong, I thought – but the mill ... I stood up and looked at the sack-men struggling with their wriggling sacks. They were too busy to speak to me, so I strolled along the way they were going, and presently followed one of them through a doorway. Just inside the door a large area beside the gangway had been screened off, and from inside it came shouting and the murmurs of a large number of people. I looked inside and saw a crowd all with their backs to me, scrambling and clamouring to see something which was going on in the middle of the crowd. I could hear somebody screaming and cursing in a loud voice, and suddenly a large part of the crowd on my left seemed to be thrown back, while a loud cheer went up from those on my right.

I climbed up on to a box which was standing against the partition, and saw that in the centre of the crowd was a small space like a ring, in opposite corners of which sat two men being variously fussed over and attended to by several others. They wore no special clothes and looked very unequally matched. On the left was a little old wizened man with no eyes, no hair and one of the arms of his overall empty. On the right was a huge rolling fat man all sweaty and red in the face as if he had just lost his temper, and his nose was running until one of his attendants wiped it with a scrap of greasy rag. The crowd on my left reassembled with much jostling behind the little old man. Then they both stood up, and the old man took several deep breaths and snorked up his nose and spat a big green gobble on the floor and rubbed it in with his boot. Then he opened his mouth and shouted out the most dreadful obscenity I have ever heard, all about private bodily functions and the other man's mother, terrible it was, I felt quite physically sick. The crowd behind the other man swayed a little, while he frowned like a stormcloud and clenched and unclenched his fists. The little old man screamed out again, something even worse than before, a very short, very personal and extremely distasteful statement about some sexual relationship the other had with his children, which was all dotted about with the most dreadful obscene words. Then the old man followed up with something else about some other alleged activities of the other man, and started to make obscene gestures with his hands and body. The crowd opposite threw up their hands and staggered back, while the fat man in front of them seethed and hissed like a steam engine and blew bubbles out of his nose. Apparently unable to control himself any longer he then rushed across the ring, but the crowd behind the older man surged out and pushed the fat man back to his place, and reassembled as before with much jubilation. I gathered that the fat man had lost a point.

Both the men were sitting again now, being rubbed and whispered to by those in the crowd who were nearest them. Then the fat man wiped his nose on his sleeve, stood up, pushed two small pieces of cloth inside his ears and pointed his finger at the other man. He spoke, and his voice was like crunching coal. He uttered a stream of frightful obscenities which went on and on, growing in volume and complexity as it continued, so that soon I had quite lost track and could only make out a word here and there. All the words were characterised by loud thumping guttural noises, and hissing and bubbling S's and F's, B's and C's like gunfire, and rolling roaring R's as the man grew redder and redder and his eyes popped out like brass buttons. I wondered what on earth could be the nature of human experience which could require such words to express it. What terrible places must these men have come from, I thought, and what dreadful things must they have done? I stepped down from the box just as the left side of the crowd again dissolved into confusion.

'Strong meat, isn't it?' grinned a man next to me. 'I
wonder who's winning – it's the traditional versus the
modern, really. The fat one's much more creative, but it's
tradition that counts in this sort of thing. We should have it
on the stage of the Theatre Royal some time. Before Royalty.'
I said that I thought that the Lord Chamberlain would
almost certainly not allow it. 'Then he must be very stupid,'
the man said, 'if he thinks that what is good for our real lives
is not good enough for our theatres. They will become no
better than brothels, and our brothels will have to become
our theatres.' I said that I could not but sympathise with the
Lord Chamberlain's attitude. 'Oh, I'm sure it's a very fine
attitude,' replied the man, 'very noble and very refined. But
if he's so concerned about this sort of language why doesn't
he get up off his arse and try to find out why it is that some
people should wish to express themselves in that way, instead
of pretending that something which is part of the fabric of
the majority of people's lives doesn't really exist?' So saying
he turned back into the crowd, and I walked away sadly
through the empty shop. Lost once more, I wandered quite
aimlessly and without hope through many doors one after
the other, but nowhere was there anyone to speak to. The last
of the doors looked no different from any of the others, and
I was taken quite by surprise.

I saw before me an incredible sight. I was standing in a
hall, the biggest hall I had ever seen – in fact, I could not see
the far walls of it in any direction, and the roof was higher
than any roof I had ever been under. Through the hall passed
a great roller track which was built up about four feet above
the floor, and this track seemed to stretch to my right and left
to infinity itself. It was, of course, the assembly line, and I
almost cried out when I realised this. On the other side of the
track, stretching away at right-angles to it as far as the eye
could see, were rows of smaller tracks placed side by side
forming a huge landscape of parallel converging lines, and

each of these carried towards the main line a series of identical assemblies, each track with a different kind. Along the main line stood a row of men shoulder to shoulder with their backs to me, extending along the track in both directions to infinity, and a row of men stood on the left side of each one of the tributaries, also for as far as the eye could see. Here was such a hustle and a bustle as I had never seen, stacker trucks buzzed to and fro along the lines, men in white coats hurried from place to place climbing over or crawling under the tracks with rulers or notepads held between their teeth, labourers rushed everywhere pushing little red trolleys, loudspeakers croaked instructions or blared out music, while the men along the tracks elbowed each other in a frenzy of work, wielding spanners and screwdrivers, or mechanised nut-drivers suspended from the roof on pulleys. Slowly the great row of assemblies moved along towards my right, and slowly they grew. Between one man and the next they did not seem to change much, but if I ran my eye along a little way I could see the difference. Where one of the tributary tracks brought with it a particularly large sub-assembly I could see the difference straight away, but mostly the growth of the main construction was very slow.

I must now set about finding my pulley. I walked through the bustle of trucks and trolleys until I was standing behind the row of men on the main track. I ran my eye over the assembly which was immediately opposite. It was extremely complex and already very large indeed, and it had passed on and been replaced by another before I had scrutinised a quarter of it; but since the next one was of course identical this made no difference. I continued my examination on the next, and the next. I could see no pulley. I started again, and scrutinised six more very closely. Still no pulley. Clearly I must walk down the line in the direction from which the assemblies were coming, to a point where the thing was in an earlier stage of its construction.

I walked for some distance along the line until I could clearly see a difference in the machine: not that it looked much smaller in bulk, but I could see various gaps here and there in its mechanisms. No one seemed to be taking any notice of me, and I did not feel like an intruder at all. I turned and faced the line again, peering between the heads of the assemblers to see the bottom parts of the machine. It was still tremendously complicated, however, and I took a pencil and a scrap of paper from my pocket, drew a quick sketch of the thing and divided this by horizontal and vertical lines into twenty-five sections with the intention of examining each section minutely in turn as twenty-five assemblies passed. This would take some time, but it was, I decided, the only way.

When at last I had finished the twenty-fifth section I felt quite tired, and decided against repeating that particular examination. I put my pencil and paper away and turned again to walk down the line. This time I walked a considerable distance, and without looking up at the assemblies, so that when I finally stopped I expected them to look much smaller. They had grown a little smaller, but not as much as I had expected, so I put my head down and forced myself to walk as far again, counting the paces. Two hundred and forty-two. Now there was a marked difference. I took out my paper and sketched it again (I shall soon be an expert on this machine, I thought), dividing it again into twenty-five sections. I faithfully searched each side, but there was no pulley. I was discouraged.

Pinquean Smallcreep, I said to myself, you are within a hair's breadth of victory. Do not lose heart! It was then that I noticed one of the sub-assemblies tipping over slowly on to the main track. These were also complex, I noticed, though none of them were much larger than a couple of shoe boxes put together. If my pulley were attached to one of these it could be assembled on to the main structure and concealed.

Obviously I must watch these things, not the main track; so I craned my neck over the shoulders of the two men who had seized the device and were wrestling it into place on the main machine. They tightened a screw here and a nut there and threaded a long spindle through into the body of the machine, and then turned their attention to the next sub-assembly, which was moving on to the track on the other side of the next machine. Again I peered, as they went through exactly the same motions again, but I could see no pulley. Very well, I must look at the next sub-assembly. I turned and walked the few paces to where the next subsidiary track tipped its load, and watched two of these being fitted. Again no pulley, so I carried out an examination of four more sub-assemblies in succession down the line, but found no sign of my pulley.

Then it occurred to me that my component might arrive at this point concealed inside one of the sub-assemblies rather than attached to its outer mechanisms, and this dismayed me because if this was the case then I should have to walk down each sub-assembly line in turn, and that would take me years, and who knows but that at the other end of these subsidiary lines they were joined by numbers of sub-sub-assembly lines? With horror I remembered that on the blueprint of the pulley, which hangs in the slotting section, there is mention of a 'part-comp. sub-sub-sub-assy'. For years I had brooded over this message, and now the full horror of its meaning came to me. What hope was there in this ordered wilderness now?

I sat down on a box and covered my face with my hands, but suddenly I heard a grinding and a groaning and a rushing sound in the air above me, and I looked up to see a fearful sight. Under the roof a huge shadow was racing over us, a shadow so long that it stretched from one side of the shop to the other as far as the eye could see. It was exactly like a great bridge sliding across the roof, and suddenly I realised that it was a bridge crane. Suspended beneath it was a little box in which sat a man in an overcoat and scarf, his shoulders hunched up and his gloved fists clamped on to two levers in front of his knees. He had a large moustache, and out of this stuck a pipe from which puffs of smoke came periodically. As he swept over us like a nightmare bird, with his hooked chain flying just above our heads, I saw the tobacco-smoke curling around him and drifting about his clothing, as if he took the wind along with him. The shadow raced away up the hall, until it was no more than a pencil in the roof.

For some time I thought and thought, and watched the men go through their sequences of actions. What was it that kept them going year after year until they died, when I could not find the heart to do so? At least I had more elbow-room in the slotting section, at least I was not constantly pressed by a moving line of work. And then it struck me just what it was that kept them going, and in that instant I saw its relevance to my present situation. It has never been my habit to 'do the pools', or indeed to bet in any way at all. But I knew that the majority of factory workers, particularly those whose work is very tedious and poorly paid, invest a good deal of their earnings in these pools. I had always thought these activities rather distasteful – I can't think why, for my father would often spend as much as a pound a week on pools and think nothing of it – and at best unprofitable, but now the truth shone forth to me. The answer was faith, without which these men would never so much as put a card in a clock; faith, not in God, not in Man, not in Justice, not in Reason – for all these things many of them think to be false – but in Chance, whose power and omnipresence arc reported in every word they read. I would have faith.

I went up to the track and chose a sub-assembly line. I looked at the device on it for some time, then walked over to look at another one. Nothing to choose between them. But then, this was not a matter of judgement. I made as if to duck

under the main line between the legs of the assemblers, but
then it struck me what a pity it would be if the sub-assembly
I had just left had been the one containing my pulley, and I
had been so close. I wondered if I should go back, but then I
saw how sad it would be if I went back and then it had been
this one which I had actually been about to go to. Ah, the
sweet agony of the gambler! I stifled all these thoughts and
concentrated on my faith.

I ducked between the legs and crawled under the line,
through inches of rubbish and filth, to emerge between a sub-
line and a row of backs. I stood up and looked over the
backs, but then I realised that I was in a position to observe
both my lines, one on my right hand and the other on my left.
But my eye moved over the rows and rows of subsidiary lines
on the other side of them both, and realising that my pulley
could be on any one of hundreds of lines I was sobered again.
Faith. I moved on between the two lines, walking away from
the main track, looking to right and left. Each man stood
with a box of components or small sub-assemblies by his
side, or even a box of just nuts and bolts, and he fitted one
to each of the assemblies which passed, tightening a nut or a
screw each time. One might have thought that since the sub-
assemblies were not very big, the lines which bore them
would not be very long. But this was not so, the lines
stretched ahead of me as far as I could see, and looking at the
men I could see why. The sub-assemblies were, although
small, very complex, and yet there were rows of men one
after another who did nothing more than add a single nut or
bolt, and one or two who added nothing at all, but made
small adjustments to the tiling. Not that they weren't busy –
they were, for some of the screws and parts were so tiny or
their fixings so inaccessible, that it was as much as they could
manage to complete one before the next was in front of
them. Someone, then, was fixing my pulleys like that –
someone was picking them up out of a crate, just as I had put

them in, and putting them on to a spindle, perhaps screwing a retaining screw behind them. His fingers would at this moment be touching where mine had touched, his fingerprints over my fingerprints – surely there was the possibility of some kind of telepathic contact when such a thing happened?

Careful, now. What is to be done? I mustn't lose faith. I knew for certain, for absolute certain, that in this hall was my pulley and the answer to my problem. I could perhaps scan four or even six rows if I stood on tiptoe. When I had finished those six – or eight – I could start on another eight, or even perhaps ten, if I had time ...

Time. There was a feeling of evening already. Nothing changes in a factory, but there are feelings of time apart from the clocks. Towards the end of the day there is a feeling of waning responsibility, a feeling that schedules can no longer be caught up with, mistakes no longer rectified, a feeling of washing one's hands, of being about to wash one's hands; pieces of rag catch the eye, keys become heavy in the pocket, overall buttons feel tight and trouser bottoms ask to have cycle-clips put on them. The work does not slacken, the light does not change; but the foreman's eye closes just a little, and men may stand with their hands in their pockets. The stomach is also a timekeeper – not only in the matter of meals but of other things too, and I knew that it wasn't as late as that; but there was a feeling.

Perhaps I could find it by less systematic methods; chance helps those who take chances. I looked all around, craning my neck. Six lines away I saw something turn in a man's hand. It could be. I dodged under the tracks saying 'Excuse me' as I slid through people's legs, but when I got there they were only sprockets. One or two men were swearing at me. I craned my neck again, and saw another round thing about the right size, away over to my left. I dived under the tracks again, and this time nearly knocked a man over before I arrived. They weren't pulleys, but small flywheels. A man was shouting, ' 'Oo the 'ell is 'e, a nut-case or something?' and then he shouted to a man in a white coat. I climbed up on to a track this time, apologising to the men working there, and looked around. Perhaps this was the best method after all – I was certainly covering some ground. The man in the white coat was shouting at me, but I couldn't understand what he was saying. Yes, covering some ground. But it would take an age to cover all of it. Faith, man, faith. I spotted another component. A man in a white coat came running towards me down the line, but I was away under the tracks again. Several of the men aimed kicks at me as I came through, but I dodged under and under towards the place where I had seen the likely component before they could try again. Men were shouting backwards and forwards now, and several white coats were running towards me. No good again, a chain sprocket this time. Up I went on another track, and saw a pulley for sure this time. Two men caught hold of my legs then, but I said, 'I'm sorry, but it's getting late,' and punched one of them in the face. They let go and I jumped down, dived under a track and emerged to find myself surrounded by men in white coats. They grabbed me, but I said that I had to look at the component over there, and struggled free after kicking one of them. Under two more tracks, over another, and I snatched the component from the assembler's hand. It had no slot, and I threw it at his face.

I struggled all the way, but there were too many of them. They carried me down the lines to the main assembly track and whistled up an auto-truck. 'Dump this nutter at the end,' they told the driver, and threw me as hard as they could into the wooden skip, and I lay half-stunned while the truck roared through space for what seemed an age. At last he tipped me out on to the floor with no more regard than if I were a sack of potatoes, and turned his truck and drove away.

I sat up, to find that I was at the end, at the end of the assembly line. In front of me stood a construction which beggared all description. Its four sides faced out to the four walls of the factory, and to the four corners of the town beyond them. Looking up I saw that the top of it lay an inch below the roof, for it was as long as it was broad as it was high, and it would drive a man mad to look at it, it was so dreadful. It cast a shadow on every side of it which was like the middle of the night, it covered up the ground on which it stood, and stood up into the air in which it stood as if the air lapped at its feet like the sea and the ground was put there for it to stand on. I could not sit and I could not lie and I could not stand beneath it.

Good God, I said, is this machine what we have made, and I smelt the smells of it, of all its parts, and what we had done to them. I smelt the coolant oil, the smell of cut metal, of burning grinding dust. It reeked of sweat, it reeked of all the smells of the foundry, it smelt of the drawing office and the paint shop, of the cesspit and the toolroom, of hardening and softening, of rubber, of plastic, of grease, it stank of human sacrifice. My God, I said, is this what we have created?

A man came running then, holding a crank in his hand. I realised that he was about to start the machine, start it up, to start this thing running, a thing, a thing which up until now had been nothing but a collection of dead pieces of iron, objects cast in sand by us, shaped by us, thrown and dragged about by labourers or left in heaps where, but for us, they would stay until they rusted away to powder. To start it running on its own? If a man said, 'If you take some pieces of metal and shape them in the right way and put them together in the right way they will come to life and move about, walk, run, fly quite independently of any other creature,' people would declare he was mad. Here was a notice which said, 'Engines must not be started until all guards are in position,' and another, 'Danger – Rotating Flywheel.' The thing was dangerous, then, it would harm the very people who had brought it to life. The man was making his final check before starting the thing. He put a ladder against the side of it and ran up like an ant to peer about inside a trapdoor. Satisfied, he closed the trapdoor and ran down. Should I stop him, should I say, please don't start it, not this one? If the germ of life has been created inside this thing, I'd say, who knows what form it might take? What ideas might not get into that cranky iron brain, what schemes of senseless mechanical destruction on land, or from the air or in the depths of the sea? When you start it, it might rear up and crush us all, or divide up into small pieces to carry some evil to all the corners of the earth, or roar through the midnight streets chasing cats and overturning dustbins and bringing people to the windows in their pyjamas.

But the man was pushing levers and pressing buttons. Something moved, I saw it. The thing sneezed. He adjusted a dial and pushed another button. A deep choking cough like the first breath of a newborn whale sounded deep inside, and a dribble of mucus came from somewhere. He pressed the button again and filthy water came gurgling out of one side with a noise like someone vomiting, then again, then a loud belch, a muffled explosion, a sneeze, another explosion and another. It started them somewhere down in a dark iron hole and hurled them into chambers full of whirling chains and cannon-balls, divided them, magnified each part in concentric trumpets and roared out the result through pipes and ports and vents and manifolds proclaiming a new prophet. The machine was alive and roared out that it was alive, roared it out so that no one within ten miles should be in doubt of the fact, that holy power and might had come up from the centre of the earth to possess this heap of cold metal, that as from now something new had arrived on the surface of the earth which would have to be taken into account in any future calculations regarding the movement of the tides or the intentions of men.

The machine belched fire and smoke, and a scorching wind blew past me. The noise grew and grew to a pitch beyond anything I had ever heard before. The ground shook and hammered the soles of my feet so that I danced an inch from the ground. Still the sound grew, so that I might have been shouting and screaming and yet have been conscious of nothing more than my mouth opening and closing. The sound held me fast like a jellied eel, picked me up petrified and laid me horizontal, filleted me before my eyes and laid me out in chunks on the hammering floor. I picked myself up and stood again, to be perforated, dissolved, separated atom from atom and dispersed like a rare gas. By a great effort of will I reclaimed my fists and stuffed them into my pockets for all the difference it made. The noise was all purple and magenta, I saw it spreading out from the machine in trembling curtains of changing colour like the northern lights, and creeping like moss on the surfaces of the machine, patterns of red and mauve chasing each other round snarling spinning wheels, red balloons pouring into the air.

I wondered how long the noise could go on increasing in volume before something dreadful happened. Suddenly I felt that noise coming into my groin, it was frightening. My ears were giving way to my genitals, which heard the noise like the noise of a great orchestra. It came flowing into my body, raging into my belly as real as an intravenous injection, a dreadful energy, swelling up me like fire, boiling and surging into my chest and arms. It felt like anger, terrible anger, or the urge to rape, or build tremendous ships. My veins swelled with the noise, my hands came out in front of me and offered themselves, pleading for direction. What must I do? I peered through the noise at the machine, but it told me nothing. 'What must I do?' I believe I shouted out, but I heard nothing come out of my mouth. What can I do with arms like these?

I could tear down every clock and crush it to powder in my hands, I could stand up and bellow down the long halls, I could ravage secretaries like a wild beast. But I couldn't. What must I do? I screwed up my eyes, stuffed my fists further into my ears, tried to close myself up. I drew every muscle in my body tight to breaking point in an effort to contain the rage, but still I boiled and burned and thought that I should burst. My mind worked ferociously in the roaring darkness. I must control myself, I was hysterical. At least, I supposed I was – I'd never been hysterical before. My wife was often hysterical, but I hadn't known that it felt like this. I was always calm then, and would tell her not to behave so stupidly because all problems can be solved by self-control and the use of reason. My head was singing like a violin, so I squatted down and put it between my knees and folded my hands round the back of my neck. I drew the muscles of my face back to my ears. I stuffed my knees into my ears. No ears, no eyes, but still the noise turning slowly in coloured wheels inside my eyeballs, a fully turned on tap filling my ears like funnels, noise instead of blood, noise instead of brain, a bladder helpless with noise.

But the pulley didn't matter, no reason to get upset. My throat began to feel tight, a queer feeling like having a fishbone stuck in it. Worse and worse. Was I going to cry, then? But I hadn't cried for thirty years. My wife often wept, of course, and I'd say, for heaven's sake pull yourself together and stop crying. But I didn't know it felt like this. I kept on telling myself that the pulley wasn't all that important. I was Pinquean Smallcreep, a man who worked in a factory on a slotting machine. Slotting pulleys. Pulleys. What for pulleys? Oh, I don't know, pulleys. What happened then – did they take them out and throw them away when Pinquean Smallcreep had done with them? 'Of course not,' I shouted out, or thought I shouted out. They wouldn't do that, it wouldn't make sense. I was Pinquean Smallcreep, 1644/254.

Blue eyes, weight ten stone four, height – I couldn't remember my height, but I had been married fifteen years (or was it twenty-two?) to Marilyn Smallcreep. I have two children – two children? Soon I should retire. (Soon? How soon? Well, I couldn't stay here until I died – nobody dies at work, you went home so that your wife could help you and stop morbid people coming to look at you.)

I rotated my head upwards between my knees and opened one eye. The machine was there, raging the air rigid with noise, drenching me in thick purple noise, pickling me in raw red strips jammed in a jar, rammed down with a rolling pin, pressed down with a press. The jar would burst. I pulled up my stomach muscles until they felt like two bars of steel in a tensile test. Men in white coats sucking pencils would be making notes somewhere in the concrete air. This is 1644/254 coming up to breaking point. Observe the form taken under tension. Determine the elastic limit, the modulus of elasticity and the ultimate tensile stress. Calculate when and where the fracture will occur.

I shouted out as loud as my mouth would open and stood up. Out, out of the noise. I turned away from the machine and frogmarched myself away, but there were more machines running, a line of them at the end of the track. I was walking between them. Now the air glowed incandescent red with noise, like walking inside a fluorescent lamp, like walking under streetlamps in the smoke of the end of the world. My feet were dancing crazily under me, was I walking or running or jumping? I seemed to have reached a door, and fell through it, soaked and cold with sweat.

Somewhere overhead the straddling bridge crane was running. I looked up to see it swinging over the shops towards me. I could see the man crouching in the cage. I saw his moustache swept back to his ears by the wind, the smoke from his pipe writhing and wriggling over his head like a wig of grey snakes. He gripped the two levers in his terrible fists like a man at the controls of a great gun, and as he swept overhead I saw his bared teeth like rows of concrete blocks, and the whites of his eyes which were rolling and rolling up there in the roof. His breath left puffs of vapour hanging for a second in the cold air, and then he was gone, but his shadow came after him like the shadow of an enemy aircraft and touched me, so that I shivered, as if my name had been marked down in a book.

I walked on, and saw visions. I saw men walking in crowds through the streets of the town, walking to the factory in the cold silent dawn with their hands deep in their pockets and their collars up to their ears. They were not walking this morning or tomorrow morning but all mornings for all time past and future, and they grew old as they walked. The columns in the streets converged, so that at the entrance to the factory the humped grey men hurried shoulder to shoulder across the road, a vast blind herd of men, where they had walked a thousand times before. Inside the factory I heard 'Morning' and then the reply from those already inside – 'Morning'. As they came one by one through the doors each man said 'Morning', and those inside replied, so that this became a chanted dialogue between each individual and the growing crowd within. Each man took a card and pushed it between the teeth of the clock, which rang its bell. The hands of the watching clocks moved on towards the instant when all these lives would suddenly cease to belong to the men who lived them for another eight hours of a day, and the crowds in the streets thickened and moved more quickly, while the chant inside the factory grew louder and faster. The clocks moved on another increment and I could hear all the bells of all the clocking-in machines ringing like a Sunday gone mad. The crowd outside was running now, and men were spitting through the doors like bullets with their coats flying out behind them and their hats falling off. MORNING – Morning – MORNING – Morning –

201

MORNING – Morning, the chant was feverish and deafening. Men threw themselves along the streets in crowds like herds of mad cattle, and crashed through the doors and tripped and fell and threw themselves at the clocking-in machines. The chant had reached its crescendo and hung in the air, a continuous roar of sound which drowned the words of the entering men – and then, as the clocks moved again, the great horns and sirens spoke out, drowning the bells and drowning the chant in a howling as if all the souls in Hell had cried out in that instant.

The thing was done. Those few still in the town heard it, and stopped hurrying. The machines began to start. I moved through my vision, walking once more along the gangways and corridors. I saw the men in the workshops working together without speaking. I saw them working in acres, acres of men, and then they began to multiply, to bunch up, working shoulder to shoulder but not speaking, crammed and crowded in like sardines. They stood in a vast pancake on the side of the hill, and then I saw that it was a honeycomb, the tier of a wasps' nest, with each man standing in his cell with his arms by his sides. Some of them had little white heads like chrysalides, and they wriggled in their cells. At each of the four compass points of the comb stood a huge yawn, with its vast bones creaking and its lips stretching and its teeth rattling as the wind howled through it.

Then I saw time; and another honeycomb, which was another day, came down on the first and covered it as it lay on the side of the hill, so that the walls of the first honeycomb creaked and swayed. Then came another day, and another, sandwiching on to the first two until soon the hill was hidden by the layers. Still they came, and the structure grew up until its shadow fell across the town.

At the instant that the sun was blacked out by it I saw a vision of all that there was in the town, of all the babies that were half-born in that second, of all those in sexual orgasm, of all those dying in that precise second of time. I saw a man hanged on the town gallows while men watched from the town jail. I saw all the murderers murdering and all the torturers at work in the dark cellars of the town. I saw all the hearts pumping and the stomachs working, all the intestines pushing and squeezing the food along, all the bladders emptying and filling, all the teeth growing and all the teeth being extracted in the shadow of the factory. I saw babies howling for food and weeds growing out of the walls of the streets in the darkness, while the wind skipped over the roofs and through the streets and the wallchart children cringed in the gutters of the council estates of the town where the washing dripped on the lines and the women cleaned things irritably. In the churchyards of the town I saw the dead lying in rows in the graves, and I thought how stupid and disappointed and finally dead are the dead.

I remembered my youth, I remembered suddenly as a schoolboy seeing in the white face of a droning teacher all that lay before me as my life, I remembered the lethargy, the vague bottomlessness of youth, its petty perversions too ordinary to be anything but utterly dreary. I remembered falling in love for the first time and feeling that at last here was something splendid, something worth working for – and then the disillusion and the disappointment, all to be repeated again and again until I could not be deceived any more. And then I was deceived once more, and I remembered us masturbating each other in damp foggy passages while she watched for people coming, I remembered breathlessness and guilt and fear of pregnancy in dark streets, the hypocrisy of the wedding, I remembered the endless quarrels and bickering, and how the children pretended to take no notice; I remembered Christmases, with uncles drinking and flirting with each other's wives because they were growing fat and bald, burping at table and playing cards until midnight because they could think of nothing better to do that they dared do. I remembered my grandparents singing themselves to death day by day with their old song books, a grandfather who could not walk reading westerns while his wife read love stories. I remembered the men walking in the town with their wives clutching at their arms, meek as mice and smart as clerks, walking little steps past the shops and the bank and the cemetery on a Saturday, saying, 'Good afternoon, good afternoon'.

And as I saw and remembered all these things I wished, and my bones wished till they ached, and my hands and feet wished out then, for someone somewhere to give the power to me, to give me the strength to flail up those dumb graves with my breath and kick out the dead, to drag out by the legs every corpse with legs to stand, and stand him up against the graveyard railings; and then to go round to the passers-by and jam their heads living face to dead all down the line, and then to stand on a gravestone and shout, to climb to the top of the spire and shout out down to the whole town – 'In the name of Almighty bloody God where is the glory? Where is the glory of it? Where is the song of it, where are the trumpets and the brass cymbals, where are the choirs, where are the throats which will open and pour out a sound to drown the noise of this place? Where is the joy, where are the grins, and the grins of the body, the grins of the legs and the arms, the grins of the back and the belly, of the child in the belly and of the triumph of pushing the child out of the belly; where is the thunder and lightning of human incarnation, the celebration of flesh, the celebration of clay and the feel of clay, where is the celebration of the flames in the kiln, of the muscles hammering the red iron and of all the triumphs of everything a man can put his hands to do for himself by himself and dignify himself?'

But there were only dried-up husks rustling in the draught. I picked up a pulley and set it in the machine. I pushed down a lever with my right hand and picked up a pulley with my left. I pulled the lever up, waited for the ram to rise, took off the pulley with my right hand and put the second one on with my left. I pushed down the lever and put down the first pulley. Then I picked up another pulley, pulled up the lever, took out the second pulley and put in the next. I pushed down the lever, put down the second, pulled and picked up a fourth. I pulled up the lever, took out the third and put the fourth in, before depressing the lever, putting down the completed pulley and picking up the next. I pulled the lever up again, took out the pulley and put in the next. I pushed down the lever, put the pulley down and picked up the next, then I lifted the lever, took out the pulley and replaced it with the next. I pushed down the lever ...

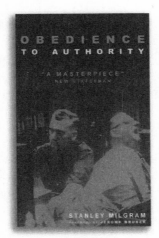

Irrationality

Stuart Sutherland

2007 | paperback | 256 pages | ISBN 978-1-905177-07-3

Why do doctors, generals, civil servants and others consistently make wrong decisions that cause enormous harm to others? And why do you sit through a boring play just because the tickets were expensive?

Irrational beliefs and behaviours are virtually universal. Not only gamblers and parapsychologists but selection committees and experts often fall into simple statistical traps to do with sample sizes or assuming causal links. In this iconoclastic book Stuart Sutherland analyses causes of irrationality and shows that it is universal. Drawing on a mass of intriguing research, he examines why we are irrational, the different kinds of irrationality, the damage it does us and the possible cures. He argues that we could reduce irrationality – but only if we first recognize how irrational we normally are.

"Terrifying, sometimes comic, very readable and totally enthralling." OLIVER SACKS

"Extremely gripping and unusually well written."
RICHARD DAWKINS

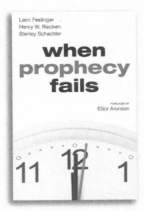